"

She didn't touch him. Or act desperate or scared or tough.

"I know exactly where we are and who I'm with. I want you. I would like to have something good happen tonight. Something I choose. I would like to remember this day not for losing an opportunity, but for taking the opportunity to connect with someone I like. Who I admire." She grinned. "Who I think is really hot."

He grinned at her in return as he pulled her down onto the bed.

"This doesn't have to be the worst New Year's Eve ever," he murmured. His mouth teased her lips, then started a downward trail as his hold on her tightened.

She pushed herself against him. An unmistakable message. His answer was in his arousal, in his low moan.

Oh, yes, this was sexy—and definitely not a mistake!

...that kind... Three short stories all in one book, which is more fun to write than you can imagine. I hope you enjoy it!

It all kicks off on New Year's Eve. Three sexy, spirited women all hoping their lives will change after a career-making audition for a hot new Broadway show. All three lives do change, but not in the way any of them dreamed.

The sparks fly when each encounters a gorgeous man.

Detective John Greco... Duty bound and forced to face the family that betrayed him. Only actress Bella can make things right.

Dr Flynn Bradshaw... Off for a much-needed vacation from his residency until he crashes into dancer Willow.

Colin Griffith... An Englishman who turns to his best friend, singer Maggie, when his brother goes missing.

All three relationships deepen as the clock ticks past midnight to bring them not only a new year, but a new life...together.

Happy holidays, and as always, much love,

Jo Leigh

SEXY MS. TAKES

BY
JO LEIGH

First published in Great Britain 2011
Harlequin Mills & Boon Limited,
Eton House, 18-24 Paradise Road, Richmond, Surrey TW9 1SR

© Jolie Kramer 2010

ISBN: 978 0 263 88054 0

14-0111

Harlequin Mills & Boon policy is to use papers that are natural, renewable
and recyclable products and made from wood grown in sustainable forests.
The logging and manufacturing processes conform to the legal environmental
regulations of the country of origin.

Printed and bound in Spain
by Litografia Rosés S.A., Barcelona

Jo Leigh has written more than forty novels since 1994. She's thrilled that she can write mysteries, suspense and comedies all under the Blaze® banner, especially because the heart of each and every book is the love story.

A triple RITA® Award finalist, Jo shares her home in Utah with her cute dog, Jessie. You can chat with Jo at her website, www.joleigh.com, and don't forget to check out her daily blog!

Once again, this is for Debbi and Birgit,
who, as always, have my back.

Ms. Cast

1

"TAXI!"

Yet another Yellow Cab passed Bella Lacarie, this one stopping half a block up for an older, well-dressed man. She kept her curses soft but vehement as she fought the urge to look once again at her watch. She wasn't late. Yet. But the traffic was insane. Yes, it was New Year's Eve Day, but it wasn't technically a holiday until tonight, and that meant midtown was a mad mix of jostling pedestrians and unruly vehicles all coated with black slush.

Another cab came, numbers lit, and this time she stepped right into the gutter, threw her right hand in the air and whistled with her left. The combination worked, and the taxi pulled up, spraying her coat with a fine mist of mud.

"520 Eighth Ave," she said, climbing in, then immediately spilled the entire contents of her tote bag on the floor. She would *not* take this as an omen. For all she knew, spilling an overloaded huge purse was the best luck ever. Still, it was hard not to sigh as she bent to collect her belongings.

Just as she picked up her hairbrush and lip gloss, she heard the driver's door open and a man yell, "Get out!"

"What the hell?" came a high-pitched, accented voice that had to belong to the driver. "Who are you? What do you want?"

Fear froze Bella as she listened to the scuffle.

"Don't shoot, don't shoot!"

Oh, God, that was still the driver. The taxi rocked. She reached for the door handle, but before she could grab it, the cab shot forward, throwing her back.

She stilled where she landed. If she sat up, the assailant would see her. He had a gun. He'd shoot her. But she wasn't all that well hidden, and the floor was big enough to hold tote bags, but not bodies.

Okay, she had to breathe. Stay quiet. He'd get where he needed to go and then run away, because the cabbie would certainly call the cops, right? So no reason to panic. Especially if she couldn't identify the man behind the wheel.

The cab turned a sharp corner, sending her and everything on the floor into the door. She squelched a cry, but not completely. Oh, God. The only good sign was that she wasn't seeing a montage of her life flash by.

He sped up, cursed, then said, quite calmly, "This is Detective Greco. My car's been disabled on Church and Leonard, it'll need a tow. I'm currently in pursuit of—"

Bella bolted upright. *"Detective?"*

The car swerved into oncoming traffic and the detective cursed her roundly as he struggled with the wheel. "What the hell?"

"You're a detective? A police officer?"

He looked at her in the mirror, his brown eyes wide, then he cursed again and took a hard left that sent her back down onto the seat.

"Hey!"

"Where'd you come from?" he asked.

"I was here," she said, sitting up again, "when you hijacked the cab."

"Great. Jesus. Just great."

"I'm not thrilled about this, either. Let me out."

He said nothing, just stepped on the gas, narrowly missing another car.

She clutched the seat. "Detective! Let me out."

"Can't."

"What? You have to. You can't take an innocent person on a car chase." Besides scaring the crap out of her, she was pretty sure this was illegal. She stared at the back of his dark head, wondering if she should try to knock him out, although that might get them both killed. "Did you hear me?"

"If I stop, I lose 'im."

They drove way too close to a black SUV and she squeezed her eyes shut, waiting for impact. Seconds later, she opened her eyes. "Can't you radio for help?"

"Yeah." He snorted. "I will. I just can't lose him. Hold on." He took a sharp left, cutting off two other cars, and throwing her against the door.

She groaned at the force of the door handle jabbing into her side. That was going to be a nice bruise.

"The scumbag is going to jail if it's the last thing I ever do," he muttered. But at least he flipped open his phone.

"I don't need it to be the last thing I ever do. Pull over."

The detective didn't seem to hear her. "He's right over there. In the old Caddy. Bastard isn't even stopping at the lights."

"Detective Greco, I'm going to have you arrested if you don't let me go." She looked in her tote, but of course, her cell wasn't there. "Now."

"Look, ma'am, I'm sorry. I'll let you out. I just need to—"

"The only thing you need to do is stop this car." This was the most important audition of her life. It could change everything. She'd worked very, very hard for this chance, and she wasn't going to let anyone blow it. Not to mention get her killed. She lifted a shaky hand and shoved the hair away from her face. "I mean it."

He cursed again.

"Yeah, that's going to help."

A MINUTE LATER, John pulled the car to the curb, trying not to go ballistic as he grimly watched Sal get away. The prick had been right there, and if he hadn't slashed his tires...

His passenger hadn't even opened her door. He looked at his phone, but calling in was useless. Sal would be long gone by the time another unit could be dispatched. He turned to his unwilling passenger only to find her bent over the backseat. Great. Now he'd have to pay to get the cab cleaned. He didn't hear anything, though. "Ma'am?"

"What?" she asked, surly as hell.

"I've pulled over."

"Your reckless driving tossed my bag all over the floor. You'll sit there and wait while I get it picked up."

He turned back to the wheel. Anger flared again as he realized he'd have to come up with a way to explain all this to the captain. As a rule, they frowned on cops commandeering a working hack to go in pursuit. Especially one with a passenger on board.

"Dammit, I can't find my cell phone. Look under your seat."

She didn't sound like a native, but her attitude was pure New York. "Yes, ma'am."

He bent, awkwardly, and fished around for the cell, knowing he wouldn't find the damn thing. Not the way this day was going. "Nothing."

"My whole life is on that cell. It has to be here."

"What's the number?"

She was silent for a moment. Then she gave it to him, her voice slightly mollified. Maybe even impressed enough not to report him.

He dialed and a tune rang out. Jesus, the opening notes from *A Chorus Line.* Shaking his head, he turned to give her a hand. That's when he saw the gun. Sticking in through the window. Pointed at her.

John dropped his cell and went for his weapon.

"Uh-uh, Johnny. I don't want to hurt the pretty lady, but if I have to, I will."

John stared at the beefy man, slowly showing him his hands. Clearly he knew who John was, but John didn't recognize the guy. He wasn't from the neighborhood, even though he had a trace of an Italian accent. Was this even about Sal? Or another case John had been working on?

"You wanna go down with Sal?" he asked the man, who smiled calmly as if he knew John was fishing.

"Pass me your gun. Nice and easy."

Shit. John picked up from where he'd left it on the seat and slowly handed it over his shoulder.

"Excuse me. Sir?"

His passenger's voice was remarkably steady, given the circumstances. John finally got a good look at her. She was pretty, all right. A damn knockout. Long, silky, brown hair. Red lips, pale skin. But her eyes, they were light blue, aquamarine. Doe eyes with dark lashes.

She turned to the guy with the gun. "I don't know this man," she said. "I'm just trying to get to Eighth Avenue, so if you don't mind, I'll just slip right away and leave you two to work this out."

"Sorry, doll. I can't let you do that."

The woman faced John again. "You've got to be kidding."

"Let the lady go. Whatever this is about, she has nothing to do with it."

"No can do, Johnny." He opened the back door and stuffed himself into the rear seat, forcing the woman to slide over. She reached for the door handle, but the guy's thick hand stopped her. "Unless Johnny here does something stupid, you'll be fine. So sit back, relax, and before you know it, you'll be where you need to go."

"I'm already late for an audition. This is a callback for me. I'm so close. I know the director wants me and I'll be the lead ingenue. Please, try to understand my position."

The big man sighed, and Johnny could swear he smelled garlic. "You seem like a nice lady, but I don't got a choice here. Shut up and you'll be all right." Keeping his gun pointed straight at his target, he said, "Drive."

"Where?"

"Just go straight till I tell you to turn."

John put the car in gear and took off, slowly, down the street, trying to think of a way to get Blue Eyes out of this. "You wanna be in the cell next to Sal's, is that it? So he won't be lonely?"

"He's not goin' to jail, Johnny, and neither am I. Turn right."

"Sal's crazy if he thinks I'm gonna let this go." John's mind raced. The guy hadn't denied knowing Sal. But how? What had that idiot gotten himself into?

"Yeah, well, we'll see who's crazy. Take the second left."

John's gaze darted between the road and the rearview mirror. Maybe there was something familiar about the guy's thick black brows and the droop to the left side of his mouth. But John still couldn't place him. Shit, he'd probably seen him in a mug shot.

"Another left at the light."

John's hands tightened on the wheel as he realized where he was heading. "What is this? Some kinda joke? You takin' me to the neighborhood?"

"You're really a very attractive girl," the man said. "So what are you, an actress?"

Bella, who'd held her breath at every bump and turn, terrified the gun would go off, looked up in surprise. She'd hoped the detective and the maniac would get so caught up in the conversation that she'd have an opportunity to get out of this stupid car. "I do my best," she said, channeling the ballsy babe she'd played in her last stint off Broadway. "But you gentlemen seem determined to keep me away from the biggest audition of the year."

"Given this is the last day of the year, that can't be too bad, right?"

"It was an expression, somewhat hyperbolic, but close enough."

"Hyper what?"

"Never mind. What is this neighborhood you're dragging me to?"

The man gave her an oily smile instead of an answer, and met John's eyes in the mirror.

"Is this neighborhood in the city?"

"It's not far."

"Then you'll let me go?"

He shrugged. "It's not up to me. What's your name, sweetheart?"

"My name is inconsequential. Just think of me as the innocent bystander. The one who's done nothing whatsoever that would cause anyone to shoot me."

He laughed. At least she thought it was a laugh. It could have been a cough. The man had a very thick neck, topped by a couple of chins. His face had that ruddy, unhealthy look, as if one more plate of spaghetti would send him to the hospital. Counseling him on his eating habits probably wasn't a good idea. She just hoped he didn't have a stroke before he stopped pointing that gun at her.

"You can call me Vince," he said, his gaze going to her chest.

She pulled her coat closed.

"Where you takin' us?" The detective glanced back at the big man. "A warehouse? That field by Tony's? You don't want to kill a cop. That's life, buddy. Hard time."

"Shut up. I'm talkin' back here."

"No, no," Bella said. "Feel free to discuss whatever you want. I'm not even listening. I'm humming quietly to myself." She bit her lip. Why did she have to babble when she was nervous? If she'd just stay quiet, do what he asked… Oh, God, if she could just not throw up…

"You're damn cute." He lifted the gun a bit. "Where are your people from, huh? France, maybe?"

"My people are from Arizona. Tempe, to be exact."

"Naw, I'm talkin' about your *famiglia,* your ancestors."

She wasn't going to tell this cretin a thing. Not a true thing, at least. But she didn't want to piss him off, either. "Yes, France and England. That's where my ancestors are from. Are we almost there?"

He looked front, and she stole a glance at the door handle.

"Turn right, next block."

The detective started swearing a blue streak. "You're takin' me to Sal's house? Where his mother and his grandmother live? Right under his roof?"

"Pull into the garage. It's empty. Oh, and Johnny, you better hand me your cell phone, 'cause this ain't no joke."

"No, shit. I kind of figured that out when Sal shot me."

Bella tensed again, and was pretty certain she was going to be sick all over her best dress. They were taking her to a man who'd already shot a cop, who had no qualms about letting his family know. Maybe if she fainted, they'd take pity. She was good at fainting. Best in her class.

With the gun pointed at her like that, she couldn't act anything but terrified.

2

BEFORE HE'D EVEN PUT the cab in Park, the garage door closed. In the dim light, John thought about how he was going to get the actress clear so he could shoot Vince with the gun he had stashed in his ankle holster.

The door that connected the garage to the old two-story brick house opened, and there was Sal himself, pointing not his beloved Sig Sauer but a friggin' double-barreled shotgun.

"Put your hands out the window, Johnny. On top of the car."

"You know what you can do with that shotgun, don't you, Sal?" The idiot kid always had to have the biggest toys. John couldn't believe he'd given Sal the time of day, let alone tried to help him get into community college. Sal took after his mother's side. He was as thin as a rail and dressed like an extra on *Miami Vice*.

"Just do as I say." Sal's gaze went to the woman. So did the barrel of his shotgun. "Who the hell is she?"

"Put the fucking gun down before you shoot somebody." Vince sounded exasperated, and to John's surprise, Sal backed up a step and lowered the shotgun.

Which made John even more curious about Vince because the kid was too hotheaded to back down for anybody. Behind him, John heard the door opening, felt the cab rock heavily as Vince got out, then the door shut again. A moment later, his peripheral vision caught the hostage walking toward Sal. Handcuffs held her wrists behind her back and even in the puffy down coat, her arm was dwarfed by Vince's burly grip.

"Johnny. I ain't got all day."

He should refuse. Dive down and get his other gun. Shoot and pray he didn't hit the girl. But she hadn't done anything except turn up in the wrong place at the wrong time. He really didn't want to go to hell for killing her. Not that he wasn't going anyway, but still. This was all his fault, not hers.

He put his hands on the cab's roof and watched as Sal slyly inched the shotgun toward him. John stared him down, holding the kid's hateful gaze. No way John would give him the satisfaction of showing that he gave a damn about the shotgun. But then Sal swung the barrel so it pointed at the woman. Not just pointed. Touched. John knew exactly what would happen to her if those two shells went off.

Vince came back to the cab and cuffed John's wrists. John stood still as a statue as he was frisked, as his gun was pulled from his ankle holster. Vince snickered, and it took all John's willpower not to knee the fat man in the groin.

Vince had everything now. John's weapon, both cell phones, even the girl's tote bag from the backseat. All neat and tidy. John had to wonder how this would have played out if she hadn't been in the cab. Someone would have died, and it wouldn't have been him.

"Let's go," Vince said, poking him in the back with his pistol.

"Va fungule sfacime."

"Watch your mouth," Sal said, snorting. "Remember your girlfriend here."

"Let her go, Sal. She ain't involved in this."

"She is now, Johnny. Come on. We have things to discuss."

"Like how you shot me?"

"Be careful," Vince said, his voice lower, closer.

"What?"

Vince hissed at him. "Just shut up. It'll be okay if you just shut your mouth for five minutes."

The urge to mess up this *gavone* was so strong it made every muscle in John's body tense. He kept his gaze on the shotgun, jerking forward when it met the woman's coat.

Vince noticed and gave Sal a warning look. The whole thing made John nervous. Sal had been getting in trouble for a while, but mostly small stuff. Vince not only wasn't from the neighborhood, but he sounded as if he was from the old country. If Sal had somehow gotten mixed up with the Mob, this wouldn't end well.

And thanks to John, the woman was now in it up to her pretty little neck.

Sal pushed her inside, but not far. The door to the basement was open and he prodded her down. Vince did his own urging and soon they were in the basement of the Molinari family home, only things had changed since John had last been there.

For one, the new door at the base of the stairs. It looked weird. Not just because it was steel, but because it had a slot in the middle, as if it had been made for a psychiatric lock ward. It had to have cost a fortune, but Sal had probably gotten a deal from his uncle's cousin Nick, who owned a place out in Jersey. Or maybe this was a new Family addition. "What's with the door?"

Vince poked him on. "What did I say about keeping your mouth shut?"

"Be happy to help you with that there, Johnny," Sal said, forcing all of them inside the room.

A brown velvet couch dominated the basement itself. The TV was gone, so was the table it used to sit on. No books. No radio. Only a dingy floor lamp. The place looked like a tomb.

"Sit down."

Johnny stood his ground. "Take the cuffs off."

"Yeah, right. Sit down." Sal didn't push at him, but he did push the girl. The fear on her face when she turned was enough to get John moving.

The couch was even bigger than he'd guessed. He sank into the lumpy cushion. "So, I'm sittin'."

"You and me, Johnny, we have a deal to make."

"The only deal I'm interested in is the one where you and your mook friend here end up doing five to ten."

"Okay, so we won't talk now. That's cool. Sweat it out. I don't give a shit."

John heard movement upstairs, reminding him where he was. "Where's Nonna?"

Sal shifted nervously. "Don't worry about her."

"Jesus, Mary and Joseph, Sal, you didn't hurt her?"

Shock and then anger contorted Sal's features. "Fuck you, Johnny. What do you think I am?"

"Good question. I don't know anymore."

Sal made a move toward him. Vince stopped him. "Enough already."

"I want to talk to her." John pushed himself forward on the couch. "Right now."

Sal made a one-armed gesture. John hit him with curses that would make Nonna, who was ninety-two last San Gennero's, light enough candles to torch the Bronx.

"Sal." Vince motioned with his gun. "Get out."

"The cuffs," John said, preparing his posture to charge.

Sal didn't answer. Instead, he walked backward, the shotgun still pointed at the woman, until he reached the door. The two men slipped outside and closed the door so hard the reinforced frame shook. A moment later, the slot opened, and Vince said, "The girl first."

John stood, and so did she. He cocked his head toward the door. "It'll be a lot more comfortable."

"I'm not getting out of here anytime soon, am I?"

He winced at the fear in her eyes. "Not yet."

She looked at him a few more seconds, then went to the door and turned to offer her wrists.

A minute later it was John's turn. If he thought it would do a bit of good he'd grab Vince by his goddamn jacket and smash his face in the door. Instead, he decided to leave that option for later and concentrate on the woman.

BELLA STEPPED BACK AS John's handcuffs were unlocked and the door slot closed. She still couldn't believe this was happening. Of course she understood that the Mob existed, but even living in Manhattan she'd never dreamed she'd be in any way involved with them, especially not as a hostage. It should have been a good thing to have a detective with her, but he was the one who'd gotten her into this mess, so no points there.

No windows, a steel door, lunatics with guns, no phone. Her chance at stardom shot to hell. And she had to pee.

"Look, I don't know what to say." John met her eyes. "Sorry obviously doesn't cover it."

Bella blinked at him, not sure how to respond. Especially since his *GoodFellas* accent had suddenly disappeared. She headed for the other side of the room, hoping against hope it had a bathroom. Thank goodness it did. A stall shower, a pedestal sink and god-awful wallpaper, but infinitely better than a bucket.

She closed the door behind her, then locked it and promptly fell apart. Leaning against the door she tried to breathe, but only managed a few labored gasps. She shook so hard her teeth chattered and for a long moment she thought she was going to faint for real. Finally, her heartbeat calmed enough for her to take off her coat and put it on the hook on the door. One look in the mirror at her pasty face and she straightened up. She might be an innocent victim, but she wasn't going to lie down and wait to die. She focused on pulling herself together, using all her sense memories to project strength and calm. Thoughts of the audition almost derailed her. Just remembering how long it had taken her to dress, to make up, to do her hair this morning made her eyes well with tears. She'd been so excited. So certain that this was going to be her best New Year ever.

She all but had the part. The director had told her he just needed to convince the bean counters, and she'd be the lead. Nothing this big had ever happened to her before and now it was all going down the tubes. She couldn't even call to let him know why she wasn't there.

All she could hope for was to live to see January 1. She'd rarely thought about her own death, not seriously. To never have another audition. Never see her parents again. Or her best friend. She didn't want to die. Not today. Not like this. The whole situation was impossibly unfair. A regular Greek tragedy, only no gods were going to swoop in and save the day.

As she washed her trembling hands she tried to find something to hold on to. He was a cop. A detective, although she didn't know what kind. Killing a cop was huge. They wouldn't do that, right? Vince had said she'd be fine. Sal had said they needed to talk. If the plan was to leave no witnesses, they'd be dead already.

She did a relaxation exercise she'd learned from yoga class. No Greek gods were going to save her, and more than likely the cop wasn't, either. Which meant she'd better get on with it. Save herself.

First, she looked in the vanity drawers. Surprisingly, next to several unopened toothbrushes was a half-full box of condoms. A shudder stole through her at the thought. No guns or knives or even razor blades. She did find a hair brush that looked reasonably clean, a box of bandages and some superglue, but none of that would do her any good.

There was nothing in the trash, nothing in the shower but soap and shampoo. The towels might have helped to strangle someone, but they were awfully thick, besides, the only person she could get close to was the detective.

Finally, though, she had to leave the safety of the small room to face the reality out there. She opened the door and walked right smack into the detective. She yelped and he grabbed her by the shoulders. With her heart thudding like a bass drum, she looked into the man's dark eyes, but he seemed as surprised as she was.

"Sorry," he said. "I didn't mean to—"

"What in hell are you doing?"

He licked his bottom lip, then glanced quickly to the toilet.

She felt herself blush and she looked away, her gaze landing on his chest. He let go of her shoulders and she realized just how tightly he'd held her. He was stronger than she'd imagined, which was a good thing. Now if he was half as capable.

He rushed inside the bathroom and closed the door behind him, making her blush deepen. If this were a play, he would clearly be her hero, but in real life, heroes were in short supply. She walked away from the door, rubbing her arm. It wasn't sore, not really.

To her amazement, her stomach grumbled, and she looked at her watch. No wonder, it was after two. The auditions were still going on, and she had no doubt some other ingenue had caught the director's eye. It had been too good to be true, anyway. As if to mock her, a wave of nausea hit hard and she pressed a hand to her belly.

Trying to take her mind off of the play, she wandered around the sparse room, wrinkling her nose at the layer of dust lining the baseboards. Thank goodness the bathroom had been clean because the rest of the place needed a good vacuuming and…

On the floor next to the couch was a dirty plate topped by a crumpled paper napkin. Her repugnance was cut short as she noticed a silver handle peeking out. A knife? Please, God. She hurried over and used the toe of her shoe to move the napkin. It was a fork. Better than nothing. She could keep it tucked in her waistband. She bent to pick it up.

"At least the towels are clean."

Bella straightened and spun to face Detective Greco, and then quickly moved away from the fork. The sudden movement reminded her of the nasty bump she'd suffered in the cab. She didn't think there was any real damage to her ribs, but it hurt.

"Sorry, didn't mean to startle you. Again."

"I—" She forgot her snippy retort as it hit her how improbably handsome he was. Black hair, cut rather short on the sides, but longish on top. Thick black eyebrows that totally worked over dark brown eyes. His jaw, already peppered with a five o'clock shadow that didn't hide his cleft chin, was square and strong. Her gaze moved down past a broad chest to narrow hips. His dark suit had been cut well, and his taste in ties wasn't horrible, although wardrobe would have picked out something in red.

"Uh, ma'am?"

That brought her right back to snippy. "Just how old do you think I am?"

It was his turn to be startled. "I meant no offense."

"I'm twenty-five. I'm not married. I'm not anything but trapped here with insane mobsters and…you." Her voice cracked. "That guy, Sal…you seem to know him. Are we going to—" She cleared her throat. "I don't want you sugar-coating anything."

His lips curved in a sad smile. "Look, if I'd known you were in the back—"

"We had that discussion. I don't accept your apology. Aside from losing my audition, I'm probably going to be killed in this stupid basement. With you. I don't even know you."

His jaw flexed. "What's your name?"

"Bella."

"Bella?"

She looked at him. "What's wrong with Bella?"

"What's your last name?"

She didn't want to tell him. But she supposed he'd need it to notify her next of kin. "Lacarie. Why?"

"Listen to me, Bella Lacarie." He took her hands in his then met her gaze, his dark eyes serious. "Nothing bad is going to happen to you, understand? I'm sorry about your audition, and for getting you involved in this mess. I'd change things if I could, but I can't. What I can do is protect you here and now. You have my word, on my mother's life, that you're safe, and you'll continue to be safe. Are we clear?"

Bella felt the knot in her stomach tighten, but not from fear. She stepped out of his grasp, paced to the other side of the room and thought about his promise. She wanted to believe him. She did believe that he meant what he said. Still, she'd grab the fork as soon as his back was turned.

3

JOHN STUDIED HER REACTION. He needed her to trust him. She was clever, he could already tell that, but he needed her to be quick, too. Terrified people often made bad choices at the worst times. Knowing Sal, he was terrified, too, and he made bonehead choices in the best of circumstances.

Bella folded her arms across her chest and continued staring at him. A little pink came to her cheeks, but she didn't look away. Finally, she nodded. Once.

Good. One problem solved. Bigger issues remained. Like how he was going to get them out of this.

"None of this makes sense," she said. "Why would the Mafia want to make a deal with a detective? Why didn't they just kill you when you went to get in your car? Or when we were in the garage?" She looked at the door. "Was that…?"

John followed her gaze, listened, but he didn't hear anything.

When he turned back she was staring at him again, waiting for his answer. "Just because they're Italian, it doesn't mean they're Mafia."

"You're right. The kidnapping and the guns mean they're the Mafia."

"Good point, but not accurate. Sal's a wannabe. He

watched *The Sopranos* when he should have been going to school."

"Which reminds me. Who's Nonna and how do you know she lives here?"

He shrugged. "She's part of the neighborhood. Everybody knows everybody."

"What about Vince?"

John hesitated. He owed her the truth. "He isn't part of the neighborhood, and I don't know what he's doing here. My gut tells me he doesn't want us dead, but I'm not certain."

"Okay. Thanks for being honest." With a calm he wasn't buying, Bella headed toward the couch. "Even if they're not officially in the Mafia, they still have to deal with me. If they buy you off, I'm a witness. I was kidnapped at gunpoint. I leave here, go right to the cops and report it." She sat on the ugly couch, almost lost on the cushions.

He hadn't realized how tiny she was, probably because she was tall. But she was slender, small-boned. "I told you, they're not going to hurt you."

She sighed, looking miserable. "And you were doing so great in the honesty department."

"I'm not trying to placate you. As long as we're here, we'll be okay. If they'd taken us to some deserted warehouse, I'd be sweating it." A half-truth was better than scaring her out of her mind. He was still sweating it, all right, only because he didn't remember who the hell Vince was. This had something to do with Sal, and as much as John wanted to kick the kid's ass right now, deep down he knew Sal wouldn't hurt Nonna. And he wouldn't be stupid enough to pull anything in her basement. As far as Vince was concerned, he didn't strike John as part of one of the local crews. Smarter than Sal, but then, who wasn't?

He glanced over at Bella again, who was nervously licking her lips. "They leave any water for us?" he asked, glancing around the room.

"I didn't see any," she said quickly, stiffening.

He frowned at her odd reaction. Of course she was tense, but there was something else... Maybe not. Maybe he was just jumpy, considering she was his responsibility and anything that happened to her would be on his head.

Even with her strained smile, she was really pretty. "Maybe you could ask them for some?"

"Sure." Fair enough request, but no, something was off with her. He left the couch and at the door, yelled for Sal. He didn't get a response, but the steel was so thick he wasn't surprised. His fist alone wasn't going to be enough. He needed something to hit it with, something that would carry.

"Here," Bella said.

He turned to see she'd apparently come to the same conclusion and had taken off one of her high heels. It wasn't quite a stiletto, which was a pity. That could've done some damage to Sal's thick skull. Yet it wasn't her shoe that had snagged his attention. She crossed her leg to remove her other shoe, and the view was real nice. So was watching her walk to him in her bare feet.

"Thanks." He took the offered heel. "I break it and I owe you a pair."

"Damn right." Their eyes met, then he saw her throat convulse. "As soon as the stores open tomorrow."

"On New Year's Day?"

Fear lurked in her eyes, but she lifted her chin. "The day after, then."

"Day after tomorrow. Check." He smiled and touched her cheek.

She didn't flinch, only blinked and nodded. Poor kid. She was handling this better than he had any right to expect.

He turned back to the door. "Sal," he yelled again, and then used the heel to give the door a couple of hard whacks.

Within a minute, he heard someone thundering down the stairs. "Jesus, Johnny." It was Sal. "Can't you just shut the fuck up?"

"We need water, Sal."

"Use the damn tap."

"Come on. Don't make the lady drink that crap." John heard more movement on the other side, then Vince's deep murmuring.

"Hey, Vince, that you?" John glanced at Bella and winked. She was a bundle of nerves and probably wouldn't eat, but he wanted her to have the option. He also needed her to calm down. "How about some food, maybe a bottle of vino, huh?"

Sal cursed loudly.

"Yeah, okay. We can do that," Vince said after a pause. "Hold on."

"Are you serious?" Bella said as soon as they heard the men leave and returned to the couch. "You can eat at a time like this?"

He shrugged. "Maybe. More importantly, if they'd planned to kill us soon, they sure wouldn't worry about feeding us."

Her perfectly arched brows rose. "Ah." For the first time, a hint of a smile tugged at the corners of her mouth. "Good to know."

"Not that I think they plan on killing us at all," he

said quickly. "You have to believe that. Oh, here." He handed her back her shoe.

She sighed. "I was looking forward to getting a new pair."

"Consider it done."

"Be careful of making promises you can't keep, Detective," she said grimly, and bent to slip on both shoes.

His gaze followed the perfect curve of her calves and he wondered if she did some dancing as well as acting. He almost asked, but then thought better of reminding her that he'd totally screwed up her important audition.

Another few minutes and someone was back at the door. It was Vince, not Sal. Good. Except he was more careful than Sal might have been, making John and Bella wait in the bathroom while he hastily set down a box and a couple of bottles of Chianti just inside the room before again bolting the door.

John ran to the door. "Vince, wait." Dammit, there was something familiar about the guy. Where the hell had he seen him before?

"Patience, *il mio amico,* no one has to get hurt. *Capice?*"

John glanced at Bella, her hands tightly clasped. "Just tell me where Nonna is."

"Playin' bingo." The man paused. "She made cookies. They're in the box. Now shut up, Johnny. Last warning," he said, his voice trailing as he'd begun to climb the stairs.

It wasn't the accent that was familiar. It was… Shit, he couldn't remember.

"Admirable that you're worried about Nonna," Bella said, coming closer. "But jeez, we're not exactly sitting pretty here."

"Yeah, I'm worried about her, but if she knows we're down here that tells me something, too."

"She won't let them kill us?" Bella said hopefully.

John smiled. "Something along those lines." He peeked in the box. There were amaretti cookies, a loaf of bread, some cheese, two glasses, a knife. Plastic. Interesting that Vince had brought two bottles of wine, though. Probably figured if they got him drunk, he wouldn't be so apt to kill them both. "Her cookies, that's another matter. I wouldn't touch them. Those suckers could take you down in minutes."

Bella's lips parted in surprise, and then she smiled. That made a knot deep in his chest unwind. "Are you sure you don't just want them all to yourself?"

"Sadly, no. They really are terrible. Don't get me wrong, she's a great cook, even at her age, but a lousy baker."

He filled a glass with wine, handed it to her and then took the other glass and bottle with him to the couch, hoping she'd follow. A few glasses of the Chianti might just keep her smiling. He hoped so. Not only would it mean she was relaxing, but it was nice. Her face changed with it. She must be good on the stage. A chameleon.

He waited until she sat down, got comfortable and took a sip, or rather a gulp. "You need to know, Sal's got his problems, but he's not a killer."

"He shot you."

John paused before he poured a small amount into his glass. "He didn't intend to kill me."

Bella shook her head, and he knew she didn't believe him. Why should she? But he'd be damned if he'd tell her the entire humiliating truth. In fact, before she could question him further, he went for the distraction. "Lacarie. That's what, northern Italian?"

"Yep."

"That's it? No story, no family history?"

"My family isn't like that. My folks are third generation, and they assimilated long ago."

"They named you Bella. You could have been called something boring like Jessica or Tiffany."

Her stare turned icy. "My first name is Jessica. I use my middle name because of my job."

John cleared his throat. "Jessica's nice. Bella's better."

She took the bottle from his hand and refilled her glass.

"I can't imagine what it's like not to be steeped in the culture," he said. "Around here, it's everything, and has been since the early 1900s."

"My father is an attorney, Mother volunteers and my sister, Andrea, is a stay-at-home mom. They belong to the country club and they donate to conservative causes. They're as Italian as their new Mercedes."

"You weren't curious about your heritage?"

"I try to catch the fashion highlights from Milan."

He smiled. "Do me a favor. When you meet Nonna, lie."

"What, she'll have me shot for being a bad Italian?"

He shrugged. "Maybe not shot."

"Well, that's one of them."

Sighing, he pretended to take another slug of wine and when he put it down he made sure Bella was looking him in the eyes. "Hand to God, I don't know what crazy plan they've cooked up, but it doesn't include us being shot."

From what he could see, Bella wanted to believe him. All she needed was a little more wine and he could relax about her doing something stupid while he came up with a plan.

"We okay now? You feel better?"

"Marginally."

"We're gonna get out of this, and you're gonna be fine. I swear."

"I believe that you believe it."

He couldn't argue with that. "You know what? I'm starving. I'm gonna get something to eat."

"Good for you."

"You don't want any?"

She shook her head. "Eating would divert my attention from drinking."

He got up, thankful at least that she wasn't going to inhibit the alcohol with food. The bread would take care of the token sips he was taking in order to keep her drinking. He didn't want her drunk, though, just less…

When had she taken off her coat? It must have been when she went to the bathroom. He liked that the silky blue dress was a shade or two darker than her eyes. And those legs. Another time, other circumstances, he'd have done something about it.

"Is there a problem?" she asked.

He looked up. "No. Just… No." It was definitely time to put something in his stomach. Maybe then he could figure out what his next move was, and stop thinking about those worried blue eyes.

BELLA SHIFTED THE FORK she'd managed to snatch off the dirty plate so it wasn't poking her in the butt. She wished she had pockets, but this would have to do. Her gaze never left John in his dark suit and white dress shirt. He certainly had nice hands. Nice shoulders, too. Neither distracted from her certainty that he wasn't telling her the whole truth.

Something was terribly off. That Sal was dumb wasn't hard to believe, but Vince seemed to be on the ball. That weird door had her concerned. She'd never seen one in a house before. Or anywhere, for that matter. The guns were as real as it got, and being kidnapped wasn't a joke. Had John lied about being shot? Or about his belief that Sal hadn't meant to kill him?

The whole plot seemed too far-fetched and weird to be anything but a farce, and yet there was nothing funny about any of it. Black comedies never ended well for everyone, and her role here was a bit player. Expendable. A red shirt on the planet Bronx.

John turned with a hunk of bread and some cheese in his hand. "The morons forgot plates or napkins. But the bread is fresh. You sure now?"

She nodded, trying to see past his handsome features to the man inside. "You married?"

"Nope," he said, as he joined her back on the couch. "I was engaged once. It didn't take."

"The women of Little Italy must be rending their garments. Letting someone like you get away."

He smiled as if he'd heard that a thousand times. "You'd be surprised."

"I am. You're young, handsome and a detective. What's not to like?"

"Plenty." He took a manly bite of a hunk of bread slathered with soft white cheese.

"For example…?"

"I haven't confessed in years," he said, after he swallowed. "I'm not going to start now."

"You drink?"

He brought his glass up from the floor. "Sometimes."

"Smoke?"

His dark eyebrows lowered. "No."

"Gamble?"

"Not with money."

"It must be women, then."

He paused with his glass halfway to his lips. "I like women."

"Too much? Or not in that way?"

He sighed, then took another bite. "I'm not a dog and I'm straight as an arrow."

"So come on. What's wrong with you?"

"If we're baring all, then you're going first."

Bella shook her head before she took another drink. "No way. You owe me. I'd never even be here if—"

"I work too much," he said, cutting her off.

"Ah, that old chestnut. It doesn't fly. Women fall in love with workaholics every day."

"And cheat when they never see the object of their affections."

"Why do you spend so much time at work?"

He looked at her curiously. "Why the third degree?"

"I'm supposed to trust you to save my life. How can I unless I know who you are?"

He took the last bite of bread, dusted his hands and reached into his back pocket for his wallet and his badge. He handed them to her. "Peruse."

She flipped open his NYPD badge and ID. Damn, he even took a great picture. She had to focus a little harder to read the print. Everything seemed legit, including him being thirty-two, but it didn't tell her anything about the man. "I'll take down your badge number in case I have a complaint. Now tell me why you live for your job." She opened his wallet. No pictures, however, there was a little foil packet tucked away.

"It's a big city. Lots of criminals."

She leaned back. "You'll never catch them—" The fork poked her right in the butt. She jumped practically on top of John and he had to do some fancy juggling to keep her wine from spilling.

"What's wrong?"

She had the fork in her right hand, but she was still leaning on him, holding on to his arm with a death grip. Damn it. "I'm sorry," she said, lowering her voice and her lashes. "I guess I just got frightened."

"Frightened?"

She nodded, while trying to come up with a way to distract him. "I couldn't help but notice that you take good care of yourself." Squeezing his arm a little, she tried to give him a flirty smile.

He returned his wallet to his pocket, careful not to disturb her hold. "You okay?"

"Yes."

"No epilepsy or tremors?"

So much for acting. She pulled away from him, careful to put the fork where it wouldn't attack her again. "No. I may, however, be a little drunk. Not to mention terrified. So excuse me if I'm not the perfect guest."

The look he gave her said he wasn't buying it. But what was he going to do? Lock her up for lying?

He picked up his glass, glancing at her in quick intervals as he took a long, slow sip. Bella had to move, just so she wasn't on the other end of his stare.

She'd played the scene horribly, yes, but what bothered her just as much was the realization that she'd felt better leaning on him, holding his arm, than she had since she'd gotten in the taxi.

Nothing bothered her so much as feeling weak and helpless. It also bugged the crap out of her that she'd turn so girly at the first hint of trouble. But it was true. She was scared and the only plan she had to save herself was a stupid fork.

She stood up, gripping her pitiful weapon tightly as

she did so. When she looked up, he was right in front of her, close. Really close.

"What, exactly, do you want to know about me?" he asked.

Bella could see tiny gold flecks in his eyes. Feel the heat from his body. She should step back, regain her personal space, but she didn't. "Why should I trust you?"

He stared directly into her gaze. "I give you my word I'll keep you safe."

She shook her head, which made her just the slightest bit dizzy. "How many times have you said 'I love you'?"

He leaned forward, just enough for her to get his scent. Not just his breath, which was surprisingly not bad, but the way he was clean. No cologne, no smell of fear. "Only once," he answered. "And I meant it."

"So you're an honorable man, are you?"

"Mostly. I've made mistakes, but this won't be one of them. I can handle Sal and Vince. You're inconvenienced, not in danger."

A shiver ran up her spine. "I'm not so sure about that."

His lips parted slightly and for a moment she thought he was going to kiss her. "I am," he whispered. "No one will touch you."

"No one?"

He smiled, and in that smile was all manner of promises of a different sort. Then he took a step back and walked away.

JOHN TOOK IN A BIG BREATH as he got some distance from Bella. The alcohol had already begun it's job on her, which was great in a number of ways. Not just to keep her relaxed, but if he didn't get too close to her, it would help him keep focused. He wasn't the kind of guy who wanted a woman to be less than her best. It was important when things got intimate that intentions were clear. No misunderstandings and no regrets. Now was no time to get sidetracked. His reassurances to her were real, but that didn't mean the situation couldn't turn ugly. He needed to be sharp, think things through. He couldn't do that with a hard dick.

So Sal, the genius, had come up with a plan. Something the family not only knew about, but had agreed to. Vince hadn't come out and admitted Nonna knew what was going on, but the thing was, it was hard to get away with anything secret in the neighborhood. That, more than anything else, encouraged John.

The family also knew there was no way in hell he was going to let the shooting go. Accident or not, there were legal repercussions. Maybe they were hoping for reckless endangerment charges instead of attempted murder. That might have made sense if he wasn't a cop. No way his captain would agree. There was too much at stake, especially in this city. It wouldn't matter that Sal was his cousin, that Sal had tripped as he'd tried to run away.

Two months ago John had caught him in a chop shop, stripping a BMW. Sal, having to act like a big man, had waved his gun around, and when some of the others made a break for it, Sal had, too. Only the idiot had tripped on a tool box and his weapon had gone off. John had been hit, the bullet leaving a minor flesh wound.

All the lawyers in the country would hop right on that big old "accident" wagon and there'd be the devil to pay.

Even if Nonna herself asked him, John would have to tell her his hands were tied. The law was the law, and Sal had shot a police officer. Which would piss off every mother in a ten-block radius. Christ, the whole damn family would be all over his ass.

He turned and looked at Blue Eyes, still standing where he'd left her. Her gaze met his, and that same sly grin was just as distracting from a distance. It would have made things so much simpler if he'd gotten in an empty cab. "What about you, fair Bella? You must have a full dance card."

She slowly shook her head, causing her hair to shift on her shoulders. "Nope. Nary a name."

"Why not? No way you haven't been asked."

She shrugged. "I have other priorities."

"Such as?"

"Whenever I'm not at my job, I'm taking classes or auditioning. When I get a break, I sleep."

"Is that so? Gee, I could have sworn you were all up in my face about that very thing not two minutes ago."

"It's entirely different. I'm not trying to save the world."

He grunted at that. Save the world. He'd be lucky to hold on to his job. One thing he did know, though, was

that he could save her. He had to. She was something
else. Not like the girls from the neighborhood, but not
like the Manhattan brigade, either.

He liked her. He didn't want to. All liking someone
did was get him in trouble. So he kept his pants zipped
around his precinct, didn't dally with the nice, or not-
so-nice, Italian girls. The farther away from the Bronx
he got, the better.

He changed the subject by setting the box of food
aside and turning to examine the area around the steel
door. There wasn't much room to maneuver. Not a nook
to hide in, not a closet. If he tried to jump them, the
second the door opened, Sal would see him. His gaze
moved to Bella, even though there was something happening in the back of his mind. "What do you do?"

"Act," she said. "Oh, you mean at my day job. I'm a
research assistant."

"What kind of research?"

She took in a deep breath, then let it out slowly, and
that poked a hole in his determination and his train of
thought. It was that dress. She had a gorgeous body, including beautiful breasts. Not too big, not too small, and
more than tempting given that he was able to make out
the small bumps of her nipples under the silky material.

"I'm a fact-checker for newspapers, magazines, and
I do research on whatever for writers of all kinds. It's interesting, for the most part, and my hours are flexible."

"Uh-huh."

"Detective?"

His gaze jerked up to her face. "Yeah?"

She nodded down, and he followed her look to see
that if he took so much as half a step he would've
tripped over the box and ended up on his ass. Well, hu-

miliation was also a good way to keep his mind on business.

She took another drink, then saluted him with her almost empty glass. "Let's hear it for the theater of the absurd. I'm actually thinking that despite your calm demeanor and reasonable arguments, that if this is my last night on Earth, I've sure picked a lousy place for it. A hotel room would have been better. Somewhere with great sheets, a flat-screen TV and room service. I'm not talking about a box of inedible cookies, either. While I don't mind Chianti, there should be champagne, don't you think? Something more dramatic and appropriate for the final curtain?"

"I agree, a hotel would have been much better. Say, at the Pierre?"

She grinned. "So what's the deal with the accent? When the goombas are around, you talk like someone out of *The Godfather.* With me, you sound like a high school English teacher."

He shook his head. "That's low. You could have at least said college professor."

Her laughter was low and sexy, just like her dress. "If I tell you something, Professor, will you promise not to make a big deal out of it?"

"I can try."

She took another sip of her drink. "I had plans for tonight. Good ones. Celebratory. With a very good-looking bartender. He's going to think I stood him up on purpose, and I'm…I'm going to be here."

"What kind of celebration?"

She opened her eyes in a dare. "The horizontal kind." Shit. Too much information of the wrong kind.

"You can make it up to him. If you need to, I'll back up your story. My badge will help."

Bella shrugged. "He'll be fine. I'm sure he won't go lacking. He never does."

"So, he's not—"

"He's a friend. One who doesn't expect too much."

"Funny thing. I was hoping for the same kind of evening."

The look she gave him could have been an invitation. She let her gaze move down his body before bringing it back up the same path. But more likely, it was that heady combination of booze and terror.

"I don't know," he said. "There's not much here, but we could make a party of it. See who can eat more of Nonna's cookies before they cry uncle."

She sank back down on the couch. "I have a feeling if I continue to imbibe I'm going to sleep right through the night. You can wake me when the big door opens." She picked up the Chianti bottle and stared at it a long moment before she poured herself another half glass.

The steel door made a noise. A scrape and a thunk, and then it was open, and Sal was inside. John reached for his gun that wasn't there, then rushed to block Sal from Bella. Sal had traded his shotgun for his Sig Sauer, but the damn thing was pointed at her, and that was going to stop right now.

He got straight up in Sal's face, the gun in his chest the only thing stopping him from taking Sal down hard.

"Back off, Johnny. I just want to talk."

"I don't talk to people who point a weapon at a hostage."

"All right, all right. Go sit down, huh? I won't point it at her, and we'll have a conversation, okay? Okay?"

John nodded and he backed up a step, then another. Watching. Waiting. Sal started to lower the gun as John took his third small step. As soon as it was no danger to

Bella, he flew at Sal, knocking the other man back into the door, one hand gripping Sal's wrist, the other at his neck.

The bastard kicked him in the shin, hard, then got him in the gonads, not hard, but it didn't take much to hurt like a bitch. He took Sal by the neck and twisted him around, pushed him toward the couch. "You son of a bitch. I ought to shoot you right now and be done with it. All I've ever done is try and help you, and what do I get in return, huh?" His hand squeezed down and Sal squealed. Then Sal kicked his heel into John's kneecap.

Pain blossomed in his gut, which hadn't recovered. He cursed as Sal slipped out of his grasp, but John didn't let go of the prick's wrist.

They spun around, and John caught a look at Bella at the door, banging on it with her fist. Then there was another fist right to the stomach, and he'd goddamn had it.

He slammed a right into Sal's face. Blood spurted out of his nose and his howl could have woken the dead. John gripped the gun with his other hand, but so did Sal.

"Stop it! Both of you!"

Together, he and Sal froze where they were, Bella's voice close and desperate. John kept his hands where they were and turned to find her just a couple of feet away. She looked fierce with the flush of anger on her face, and she held a weapon of her own. A fork.

Sal laughed. "You gonna fork me?" Sal asked, and then he laughed harder.

John stared wordlessly. She didn't look tipsy at all, just serious and brave. She wouldn't get anywhere, but still…

"You think I can't hurt you with this?" Bella moved even closer. "You like having two eyes, do you, Sal? Drop the gun and open the door, or I swear I'm gonna—"

Sal laughed again. "I think you'd better go sit down before you get hurt."

He kicked out at John again, but this time, John was ready for him. He twisted, then pushed hard at Sal to get him off balance. The two of them almost went down, but John had the upper hand, which he used to finally get the gun. He brought it up and aimed at Sal's bloody face. "Thank you, Bella," John said, not taking his eyes off of Sal.

"Oh, crap," she said in return, which didn't make sense until he heard the big door slam again.

"Put it down, Johnny," Vince said. "You, too, miss. Put it down and walk away."

John didn't lower the gun, but he did look back to see Vince pointing his weapon at Bella. She threw the fork and it almost hit Sal, making the man jump.

"The gun, Johnny."

He had no choice. Not with Bella a target. He gave up the Sig Sauer.

Vince intercepted the gun before Sal took it from John. "Goddammit, Sal, didn't I tell you to stay away from him?"

"I just wanted to explain."

Vince muttered something in Italian, his brows drawn together, dipping into a V, and John finally figured out where he'd seen him before. "You couldn't wait until tomorrow." Vince tilted his head a bit, staring at Sal. "He break your nose?"

Sal's hand went to his face, and he hissed as he touched it. "Goddammit."

John needed to regroup, to process what he now knew. He went to the couch, grabbing Bella's hand on the way. She gave him a look that could have singed his eyebrows, but she sat with arms crossed, legs crossed and spitting mad. John thought she looked great. Better than great. That fork thing, she'd meant business. She was brave, he'd give her that.

Sal went to the bathroom to clean up, while Vince shook his head. "I don't get you, Johnny. Sal's your cousin. He's family."

"He's your *cousin?*" Bella turned on John and he knew all the goodwill the Chianti had bought him was now history.

"I probably should have mentioned that."

"Oh, my God," she said. "You're insane." Then she faced Vince. "I suppose you're related, too?"

Vince pressed his thick lips together.

"Yeah, he's related," John said, which earned him a wary look from Vince. It had been four years.

Bella put her face in her hands. "I don't believe this."

Sal came out of the bathroom holding one of the big white towels up to his face. "You broke it, you *ciuccio*. I'll kill you for this."

"Shut up, Sal," Vince said. "Just tell him the plan."

Sal gave Vince a stare, but eventually, he brought the towel down. "We catch a flight tomorrow," Sal said. "To Uncle Tuccio's."

"You can't leave the country. Your passport's been flagged. You're under a felony warrant."

"It's all been worked out," Sal said. "Nonna put her foot down. She don't want me goin' to jail, but she says I gotta work for Tuccio, learn the business."

Vince didn't look too thrilled about it. "He can't come back until he's got his own sales territory and gets married."

John let out a breath, staring at the two of them. Knowing the family, he was sure that whatever passport and papers they'd rigged for Sal would get him on the plane. Working for Tuccio was actually pretty smart.

The old bastard sold wine across Europe, and if Sal took so much as a sip of the goods, Tuccio would have his ass. The kicker, though, had to be Nonna's doing. Sal had to get married? That could take a while. No woman in her right mind would marry that *giamope*.

But none of that mattered. If he let Sal go, the whole department would know. They'd think he had something to do with it because Sal was family. "I can't let that happen, Sal. You know I can't."

"That's why you're gonna stay here until he's out of the country," Vince said. "You got no choice."

"When, exactly, are you leaving?" Bella asked.

"Tomorrow afternoon."

She struggled to her feet, the couch doing its best to keep her still. "Surely you don't have to keep me until then. It's New Year's Eve, and I don't care if you go to Italy. I don't care about any of you."

"Sorry, sweetheart." Vince did look sorry, but the gun didn't waver. "You just keep Johnny from hurtin' anyone, okay?"

Sal gave Johnny as much of a sneer as his nose would allow. "He didn't hurt me. He thinks he's so friggin' smart with all his degrees and crap."

"Shut up, everybody." John stood. "Even if this works, and I can't stop you, I'm gonna charge you, Vince. Out of respect, I'm gonna leave Nonna out of this, but not you. You'll never be able to step foot in this country again. Is that what you want?"

Vince winced, but the gun still didn't move.

"Not for a wedding or a funeral, you're never coming back here. You understand?"

John tensed as he watched Vince's gun hand move. First he'd need to get Bella out of the way, but he was sure he could take that gun and end this farce.

He took a half step, prepared to move fast. Then Bella's hand was on his arm and she jerked him back, hard.

"What the—"

"Get out," she said, to Vince and Sal with her eyes locked on John's. "Both of you. Now."

The two men froze. Long enough for John to make his move. So why didn't he? Bella's hold could never have stopped him. But the way she looked at him, her eyes begging even as her back straightened with pride. That, he couldn't ignore. He stayed. He let Sal and Vince go. For her.

5

THE DOOR SLAMMED and Bella stared at the hand on John's arm as if it belonged to someone else.

"Bella?"

She looked into his eyes again. "I don't… I…" She let him go as her cheeks heated.

"I could have gotten the gun," he said softly, as if he didn't want to upset her. "I made sure you weren't in the line of fire. There won't be another chance. We're stuck in here until tomorrow. Those two will get clean away."

"Maybe they should," she said.

"What?"

"He didn't shoot you on purpose. You told me that. Or was that all bull?"

"Doesn't matter. He shot a cop, Bella. In New York."

"But you said it was an accident. Besides, it seems to me he'll be more rehabilitated in Italy than he would be at Leavenworth."

John shook his head. "And what about me, huh? How am I supposed to tell my captain that the man who shot me, my damn cousin, got away? You think he's not going to assume I was in on it? That I gave him a pass? I'm already the laughingstock of the department."

"Why?"

His gaze shifted before returning to meet her own. "My cousin shot me. That's not enough for you?"

He was hiding something. She'd been a detective once in a play and part of her research had included learning the eye movements of liars. She didn't understand the first thing about this insane family dynamic or what John's motivations were. "You can tell your captain the truth. That you were hijacked and Sal skipped the country."

"Yeah. He'll probably clap me on the back and give me a damn cigar." He shook his head as he went to the couch. "I had a good reputation before this. I was on the fast track. Now…"

She sat next to him and took his hand, not caring about the drying spots of blood left from his fight with Sal. "I can't believe this one incident is going to ruin your future. We've just met and I know you're a good detective. The people who work with you must know that, too."

"No offense, but you don't know anything about it."

"Explain it to me."

He looked at her for a long moment. Finally, he said, "It doesn't matter. There's nothing I can do about it now."

Bella sat back—actually sank back—on the couch. She still didn't understand why she'd stopped him. Self-preservation was the easy answer, but that explanation didn't sit right. Something in her had changed during those few minutes of arguing. Not about Sal, God no. And while Vince was smarter, he was still on her shit list. Her reaction had been all about John. Maybe it was as simple as her not wanting him to get hurt.

"Hell, Bella," he said, his voice low, his hand squeezing hers. "I'm just sorry you got caught up in all this. I hope you're convinced that no one's going to hurt you."

"I'm leaning that way, but frankly I won't be convinced until I'm safely at home. It would have helped, FYI, if you'd mentioned those two jerks were your cousins."

He grinned. "That's not an easy thing to admit. Besides, technically Vince is Sal's cousin, not mine."

She sighed and rubbed her temple. "I do feel better."

"So why don't you have something to eat, and I'll fill up your wineglass. We're here for the duration."

Now that she wasn't nauseous with fear, she felt she should eat something. "I'll get out the rest of the bread and cheeses while you go clean up."

He seemed a little surprised to see the dried blood on his hands and clothes. And a little pleased. He was such a guy.

NEW YEAR'S EVE IN a basement somewhere in Little Italy. Bella sighed as she broke off a hunk of bread, then laid it back on the cloth napkin it had been wrapped in. It was really fresh and smelled great. Wine, bread and cheese, a disgruntled detective, the world's most horrible couch. Sadly, except for missing the audition, it wasn't her worst New Year's Eve. Not even in the top ten.

Thank goodness there was another bottle of wine left. Her buzz was long gone, and she wanted it back. No matter what she'd told John, she was still scared. She'd be crazy if she wasn't.

The bathroom door opened and a somewhat cleaner John joined her on the couch where she'd spread the napkin. "The bread's good. They make it fresh every morning."

She held up her piece. "It smells wonderful. I tend to live on salad and chicken breasts, so having no choice about eating carbs is pretty cool."

"If Nonna saw you, she'd force-feed you for a month, at least."

"You think I need to fatten up?"

He smiled at her. "I think you're beautiful."

A little flutter that wasn't hunger danced in her tummy. "Thank you. I think you're beautiful, too."

He sighed. "Beautiful, huh? Great."

"Oh, stop. I was being fetching. You're ruggedly handsome and all man."

"That's better. If I didn't have my hands full, I'd adjust myself and grunt."

"Thanks for putting that image in my head."

"Sorry." He slumped and she could tell that he did feel sorry. For himself.

Something would have to be done. After all, she was stuck with him for the foreseeable future. More importantly, she understood. He was afraid he'd lost his chance. No one knew the feeling more acutely. She supposed his situation was worse. After all, he was a detective in the NYPD. He saved lives. Even if she'd gotten the part, it wouldn't have saved anyone's life but her own.

She studied him, not sure what her approach should be. Flirting had its merits, but in his current state she wasn't sure it was appropriate. It wasn't easy to cheer up a stranger. She had no idea what would bring him around. Alcohol seemed her best bet.

With his elbows on his knees, he bit into a piece of bread and chewed as if it were a penance. Not good.

She reached for her half-empty glass. "I think it's time to crack open bottle two."

He picked up the open Chianti and shook it. "Nope."

"Great. Now all you need to do is catch up."

He eyed his glass on the floor, still almost full. "You can have that. I'm not in the mood."

"Get in the mood. The sun's almost down, and since we won't be going out dancing, or watching the ball drop in Times Square, we'll need to entertain each other."

He didn't react.

"I know there's a sense of humor in there some-where."

"Nothing's very funny."

"I wonder…"

He finally looked at her. "What?"

"I bet I can make you laugh."

He almost rolled his eyes at her, but stopped just in time. "Don't bother."

"Is there something you can do to change the situation right now?" she asked.

"You know there's not."

"Then get over it."

His mouth opened, but no words followed.

"Seriously. People change their moods all the time. Look at me. I've lost my shot at stardom. I'm trapped in a lunatic's basement with a depressed cop. You don't see me moaning about it."

"You've been moaning since the cab."

"With good reason," she snapped. But no, she wasn't going to go there again. "For now, the only thing I can control is me. I choose not to wallow. I choose to eat bread and cheese, drink wine and try for a few laughs. I might even eat a cookie."

"Right. You're one of those people."

He wasn't making this easy. "What's that supposed to mean?"

"Nothing. Eat."

She put a bit of cheese on a bit of bread. The combination was as delicious as advertised. Another bite seconded her opinion, and she ignored the sourpuss next to her as she tried to practice what she'd just preached.

By the time she'd finished her half glass of wine, she'd made a decision. It was bold. It was crazy. But what the hell, right? She was the master of her destiny, and dammit, she was going to have a good New Year's Eve if it killed both of them.

JOHN FINISHED OFF HIS food, then picked up his wine. Being drunk, for all its hazards, seemed like a better idea than being sober. There was enough vino to help him forget everything about this screwed-up day, but he'd stop before that. Even when he was being held hostage, he couldn't let go of the job. And that made everything worse.

He watched Bella as he drank. She looked better. Not so pale, and she wasn't shaking anymore. He wished he could explain things to her. How terrible he felt causing her to lose her big chance. How he understood, because he'd lost his chance at stardom, too. His own family had effectively derailed his career. He'd had plans. Not just in the department, either. He'd given serious thought to politics. He didn't have to bother now. This stain wasn't gonna wash out.

"Why'd you become a cop?" Bella sipped her own wine and then leaned forward a bit, waiting for his reply.

"Temporary insanity?"

"Come on. I'm serious. Is your father a cop?"

"Nope. No one in my family. Mostly, the Grecos of the Bronx are in transportation. Trucking, to be exact. My father, my grandfather and some of my smarter cousins own a small fleet. Mostly milk runs from up-state."

"But you decided driving wasn't for you?"

"Never saw the appeal."

"Why police work?"

He shrugged. "I had an idea about what it would be like. A friend of mine from Our Lady of Mercy, his dad was a homicide detective. We thought it was exciting and like the TV shows, you know? As I got older and saw what was happening here, all the crime and the drugs, I decided being a police officer wouldn't be such a bad life. It's nothing like the TV shows, just so you know. Nothing."

"Very little is," she said. "If you knew what you know now, would you make a different choice?"

He snorted. "Hell, yeah."

"Really? What would you choose?"

"I'd be born to rich parents," he said. "Into a sane family. And I sure as hell wouldn't spend my days getting shot at, that's for sure."

"It's also complete bullshit."

"Hey."

"I'm the one who should be insulted. We're in a hostage situation and you can't even bother to tell the truth."

"What truth? I'm a civil servant who used to have unrealistic ambitions. I've been schooled. The end."

"If this is all it takes for you to run off with your tail between your legs, then it's probably a good thing. People might have counted on you."

John stood, wishing like hell he could get out of here. He went to the door and banged it so hard he felt it in his teeth. "You don't know, Bella. My family, they're all screwed up. I got so many aunts and uncles and cousins, and they all want something. Or they need something. I've been called to my aunt Francesca's to scare my nephew Alex into eating his vegetables. She wanted me to take out my gun. Can you believe that shit?"

"No." Bella walked over to him. "I can't believe any part of your family. I have no frame of reference for it, except for those unrealistic TV shows. There isn't one person in my family, including my parents, who would kidnap anyone for me, let alone a cop. Sal may be a first-class jerk, but even he has people who care.

"As for you, John Greco, I have the distinct feeling that this whole arrangement is just as much for your sake as it is for Sal's."

"What, they're doing me a favor by destroying my career?"

"No. They're putting themselves at risk so that you don't lose your family."

"Wow," he said. "Don't get me wrong. You're a hell of a brave woman and you're real bright, but you couldn't be further off the mark. They're all scared of Nonna, that's all. Scared she'll curse them and then she'll die. It's got nothing to do with me. I can guarantee not one person in my family considered the consequences I'd face because of this fiasco."

He frowned. "They sure didn't give a shit when the bastard shot me. I was the laughingstock of not just my precinct, but the whole goddamned NYPD. Greco's moron cousin shoots him in the ass, isn't that the funniest thing you ever heard? Shot in the ass trying to take down a chop shop. We're not talking about drug dealers or bangers. A chop shop, and my own cousin, who I helped all through high school, shoots me so I can't sit down for a month. And now this. I let the idiot get out of the country, and I can forget about promotions, let alone politics. I'm a joke. That's what my family has done for me. A joke."

Bella's eyes didn't soften. From what he could see, the story hadn't affected her at all. She didn't blink or shrug or laugh. Nothing. Until she put her hand on the back of his neck and pulled him into a kiss.

6

BELLA DIDN'T HAVE TO wait more than a second for
John to kiss her back. He took her mouth fiercely,
thrusting his tongue between her lips and teeth. As he
claimed her, his hands gripped her shoulders too tightly,
but she didn't whimper.

She understood his anger. His pain. There was a
price to be paid for living with his family, one she'd
never have to experience.

Which was worse? The disappointment when things
went wrong, or knowing no one cared?

Her parents loved her, but always from a distance.
They were much more interested in the law firm, in the
country club. Their bridge and tennis tournaments
seemed to light them up more than any of her good
grades or acting awards.

But that didn't mean John didn't have a right to be
angry. Let him hold her arms too tightly. Let him punish
her with his kiss. She could do that for him. For tonight.

He pulled back and then moved his lips to her jaw,
to her neck as his hands released her, only to press
down her back. She touched him in return, running her
fingers into his hair as he nibbled and nipped her sensitive skin.

It wasn't just altruism. She wasn't that nice. Yes, she
liked him, but kissing him had been as much for her own

benefit as his. She wasn't scared anymore. Okay, a little scared. But come on. This day hadn't just sucked for John. She'd lost a lot, who knows how much? She'd had a shot at the brass ring. She'd been scared out of her mind, embroiled in an insane plot that still wasn't over. No one knew where she was. If she died tonight…

She wasn't going to die right now. Right now, she was going to take all the comfort she could find. And try to give comfort in return.

John's mouth moved to her lips, more gently this time, the madness dampened a little. Well, that wouldn't do. She needed to feel this.

She pushed herself against him. An unmistakable message. His answer was in his erection, in his low moan.

HE SHOULD BACK OFF. Now. Before the situation got completely out of hand. He had no business taking advantage of her. Hadn't she been through enough today? She was vulnerable, and he hadn't helped anything by whining about his problems. Not after what he'd done to her.

If he'd pulled right over, the second he'd seen her in the back of the cab, maybe none of this would have happened. She'd have made it to her audition, and who knows? She could have been a star. Instead, she was trying to make him feel better. It didn't matter that she was doing it right. Too right. God, how she felt to his hands, to his cock. He kissed her again. Just one more minute and then he'd step away. Tell her why this was a bad idea.

It was Bella, instead, who pulled away. Not far. Just enough so he could taste her warm breath. "It's okay," she murmured. "I want this."

Shit. Guilt hit him square in the gut. He got away

from her, halfway across the room before he knew he was safe. "It's not okay. You're scared. You're a hostage. I may not have a future, but I'm still a cop tonight. I won't do this and have you regret it when we get out of here. And we will get out."

She lowered her head a bit and looked at him with those big blue eyes. "That's very sweet, Johnny. Seriously, I'm really glad you said every word. It makes my decision feel even better."

"Decision?"

She nodded. "Can you come here?"

He tilted his head, waiting to see what she had in mind. "Bella…"

"Come on. I won't bite. Just come here."

He couldn't refuse her, but he'd have to be careful. Remember what was important and what was right. The closer he got to her, the harder his task became. Jesus, she was beautiful. Even in the murky light of the old lamp, she knocked him out. Her hair, her eyes. That damn sexy dress and what was under it. "I'm here. Now what?"

"I want you," she said. She didn't touch him. Or act desperate or scared or tough. "I know exactly where we are, who I'm with and who's outside that door. I want you. I would like to have something good happen tonight. Something I choose. I would like to remember this day not for losing an opportunity, but for taking the opportunity to connect with someone I like. Who I admire. Who I think is really hot. This doesn't have to be the worst New Year's Eve ever. Honest. So I'll say it one more time, and then you have to make your decision. John, I want you."

The breath went out of him along with all the reasons he shouldn't. She was right. There was a chance for something good here. That they both could choose.

Something in his body must have told her what his choice was, because she was in his arms in two steps and her eyes were closing before his head even dipped. Her lips parted the second his mouth touched hers. He took his time, enjoying each second, each touch of her tongue, the hint of wine he tasted, the soft way she breathed. No need to rush. This would be a slow dip in a warm pool, and he planned on thinking of only her and how they could make each other feel good.

When he ran his hands up her back to the zipper of that blue dress, she stopped him. He wasn't worried, though. It wasn't for long. She just led him to the couch, and then she leaned over to turn off the ugly lamp.

It didn't make that much of a difference. The basement had been growing darker by the moment, and now, at least, there were no concerns about prying eyes. Besides, he was a big fan of touch. Giving and receiving.

Bella's hands found his chest and made their slow way up his shirt to his collar, where she deftly loosened his necktie. A moment later and he felt it slip away. She took care of the top couple of buttons, then pushed his jacket off his shoulders until it joined his tie.

"Your turn," she whispered.

He smiled as he decided to multitask. Taking her mouth first, he savored that pleasure for a bit. Then he moved his hands over her back, down to her waist, then back up her spine following the trail of her zipper. He reached the top of her dress and ran his fingers across the skin right above the neckline.

She must have liked that if her thrusting tongue was any indication. When he began pulling her zipper down, she continued to show her approval. He liked this game and her willingness to play it. It made him very hopeful for a long and satisfying night.

Finally, the zipper would go no farther. Now he could retrace the path on bare skin. He barely touched her. He wasn't sure, but he thought he could feel the goose bumps he caused and he knew he felt her tremble.

Mixing it up a little, he didn't hesitate at all when he reached her neck. He dropped her dress where she stood, picturing it pooled around her feet. God, he'd like to see her in the light, even if it was just for a minute. It was unbelievable to picture her in her high heels with nothing on but panties and a bra. Which he had yet to explore.

Her hands on his right wrist told him it was her turn once more. It wasn't easy to relinquish his quest, even if it was only temporary. But he let her have her way. She unbuttoned his sleeves and then his shirt, her little brushes of nail or skin enough to keep him hard without making him too crazy.

When his shirt fell, he stopped breathing as he waited for her hands to touch his chest. She didn't make him wait long. He hoped she wasn't one of those women who wanted mannequins instead of men, because he had hair. Not nearly as much as some of the apes he knew, but there was no mistaking that he was Italian.

Her hands skimmed along his chest just above his skin. No one had ever done that before and the movement felt good, if a little weird. On the other hand, her soft little gasp of delight was great. Oh, God, her palms brushed over his nipples, and the sensation went all the way down to his cock. He grabbed her wrists, so small, and held her right there while he struggled to regain his control.

BELLA SHIVERED AS HE held her steady, the feel of his strong hands holding her driving her right up the wall.

In a good—no, the best—way. Combined with his utter maleness, she was lost. It was so tempting to finish this agonizingly wonderful stripping and get down to it, but no. They had all night. There was no rush. Just prolonged pleasure, and wasn't that something. No thoughts wasted on who would go home, when to leave, what to say after. The door would open when the door opened, and not a second before.

A bed would have been good, but what the hell. A couch had its own charm.

His fingers released her and found her breasts. There was no squeezing them as if they might beep, which had happened too often, thank you. But then, John Greco was a grown man, not a boy in a man's body. She liked that very much. Loved that he could appreciate this magnificent torment.

Ah, he had discovered the lace that bordered the cups. This bra had cost a pretty penny, but she loved it, and the matching panties. Silk and lace, together again in a rare public appearance. He couldn't even see how beautiful they were, but he might deduce their charm with his touch.

Slowly, slowly, he circled her breasts with his index fingers, moving between the lace and the silk. Each rotation drew him closer to her very hard nipples. Two more trips, max, and then what would he do? Stop? Tweak?

Neither. Just as he swirled his fingertip over her left areola, his mouth went to her right, where he captured the erect bud between his teeth and flicked the tip with his tongue. Even through the silk—maybe because it was through the silk—the sensation made her rise to the balls of her feet, let her head fall back as she moaned with a pleasure so unique, so specific, she would remember it for the rest of her life.

He played her with exquisite precision, as if he had studied only her body for years in preparation for this night. "Oh, my God," she said. "If you can do this with only my nipples…"

He laughed. She hadn't even realized she'd spoken aloud. "No, don't stop."

"I thought we were taking turns."

She took in a couple of breaths, coming back from the stratosphere. "Right. Yes. Just give me a second."

That mouth of his came down on hers. It was a lovely segue. When he pulled back, he whispered, "Hey, I was kidding. We can do whatever you want. Whenever you want it. I could probably get off just kissing you."

"Oh, that's so sweet. A lie, but really sweet." Her hands snuck between them and moved down his pants. She frowned at how thoughtless she'd been. "Poor baby. You must feel so…constrained."

"I can't deny there's been some pressure."

"Let's see what we can do to ease the situation."

He kissed her forehead. Not on purpose. He hadn't realized she was moving south. Unbuttoning and unzipping as she made her slow way.

Once his pants had fallen to the ever-increasing mound of clothing on the carpet, she didn't wait another second to send his boxers down with them.

He gasped his surprise, but just waited. Her hand encircled the base of his cock and her mouth did the same to the crown.

Now *that* was a gasp of surprise.

SHE SMILED AT HIS IMPRESSIVE girth and swirled her tongue as she explored him. She was glad to find that while he was unquestionably male, he was also considerate. Everything was trim and tidy, very much the same aesthetic she preferred for herself.

"Why are you giggling?" he asked, but only after he'd cleared his throat.

She hummed to let him know she wasn't laughing at him, letting her mouth prove it.

He touched the back of her head very softly. Clearly he didn't want her to worry that he would get carried away. No problem, because she couldn't stay in this crouch much longer. She wanted to be naked, and she wanted him to take off his own shoes and socks. That was too much of a gray area for her.

She left him with a big lick all the way from root to tip.

Then she was on her feet, reaching back to undo her bra.

7

AS EROTIC AS THE TEASING had been, John hoped like hell she wanted to get to the main course. It actually hurt to be this hard, not that he was complaining. What she'd done to him. Good Lord.

"Hey, Johnny. In about two seconds, I'm taking off my heels. I suggest you be naked by then, or I'm starting without you."

Way to take the edge off. He grinned as he fumbled over his clothes to the couch. His shoes came off next, followed by his socks. He wished there were a blanket, though. He wanted everything to be perfect for Bella. No choice but to go with the flow.

She kicked him, but it was with her bare foot and didn't hurt at all. "Ah, you're here."

"Oh, yeah." He pulled her into his arms, groaning when he felt her naked against him. While he liked the touching part, he missed the visuals. Of course, that would be taken care of in the morning.

"You feel good," she said. She kissed his chest, nipped him on the right pec, making him flinch, but then she licked over the hurt.

"Okay, now we either have to get down on the couch or find a wall because I don't think I can wait."

"Uh, aren't you forgetting something? In your wallet."

"Ah, shit." Hating that he had to leave her, if only for

a minute, he found his pants and thank God he knew just where to find the condom. Sadly, there was only the one, but that was better than nothing. "Got it."

"Then put me where you want me."

She was easier to find, and he wasted no time. He swept her up into his arms, touched the couch with his shins and carefully laid her down. No complaints meant he'd judged the space well, but before he joined her, he touched her face so he could kiss her. Then he ran his hands down her nude body, loving the feel of her breasts and her skin, softer than any silk, learning her.

Carefully, he climbed on the couch, straddling her legs. He wasn't going to stay like this, but he took the time to put the condom on his aching cock.

Then he gently moved between her legs, touching her wherever he could reach. Cradled by her thighs, he put his hands down on the couch, just above her shoulders. Another kiss, this one long and sweet.

She whimpered and lifted her hips. He lowered himself so his weight was on one bent arm, and stroked her opening. She made these soft sounds and each one made his cock jump with anticipation. She was already wet, and that made him ache even more. "Bella," he said. *"Bellisima."*

"Grazie," she whispered back, as she pushed down on his fingers.

As nice as that was, he wanted more. He took hold of his cock and guided himself inside her until there was no need for help. In one strong stroke, he entered her all the way. They both groaned as he stilled there, wanting this to last.

Both her legs lifted, and he felt her heels run up his thighs until he was wrapped in soft heat. His body moved back and in, slowly at first, but she felt so damn good, he lost his control.

Her hands were on his back, pulling him closer, urging him on. Each thrust came faster and harder, but still he was able to read her, to listen to what she wanted. Her fingers in his hair brought his mouth to hers. She cried out even as they kissed, noises he'd remember forever. The darkness made it all new, magnified every sensation.

The feel of her nails running up his back. Her bare heels digging into his thighs. Her wet heat killing him with pleasure. Something shifted inside him, and the thinking stopped. Nothing existed except his cock in her pussy, his tongue in her mouth.

She broke from the kiss, gasping and meeting each thrust. He couldn't restrain himself, driven by her need to take him deeper, harder. The roaring started in his ears as his balls tightened, as he lost his rhythm and his mind.

SHE WAS GOING TO COME. Her whole body was part of it, part of the orgasm that started deep inside, that was stoked by his every touch. She was surrounded by him, and she surrounded him, and it was all too much. One second she was on the precipice, the next she was arching and crying out and trembling.

He kept riding her, jerky hard thrusts that shook the couch, that stretched her orgasm impossibly. With one last push, he stopped and she could feel his body tense as he stretched his head up with a feral cry.

Time slowed around her thudding heartbeat, as white spots flashed in front of her eyes and the sound of him dimmed with the blood rushing in her ears.

It dissipated slowly. The last thing to calm down was her heart.

John collapsed next to her, pressed against the back of the couch. One leg and one arm crossed her body. He really didn't have enough room, but she couldn't move, not yet.

"Give me a second," she said.

He grunted in reply, and she smiled, understanding. The sound of their breathing was loud in the basement and she wondered if it was midnight. If they'd shattered the old year away. Birthed the new year with their sex.

Eventually, she shifted over, turned on her side to face him. He kept his leg and arm around her, which was just exactly the right thing.

He kissed the tip of her nose. "I'm done for. You've broken me."

"Excellent," she said. "When I can move again, I'll pat myself on the back."

"No, that's my job. God, that was amazing."

"Yes. It was. Is."

His fingers rubbed against her back, the gentlest touch, but still far more than she could pull off. It felt wonderful.

"I was thinking," he said. "No way Sal could have put this whole plan together. Vince was the brains behind this. He must have come up with the idea to bait me into chasing Sal. Getting me out of my car so they could slash my tires. He had to have known that I wouldn't give it up. That I'd follow him, even if it meant taking a cab."

Bella grinned. She didn't mind. It was good for him to talk it out now, when he was exhausted and sated. "He knows you."

"But he doesn't. I haven't seen Vince in four years, at least."

"So Sal filled him in?"

His fingers stilled. "Sal? That *gavone* couldn't find

his dick with both hands. No. It had to have been a group effort. Sal's mother. Nonna. Hell, for all I know my own parents pitched in. Had to be."

She reached over and touched his temple, then stroked his hair. "It's going to be all right, you know. I may not be a police officer, but I'm a hell of a witness. I'll tell them all that you had nothing to do with the escape. They'll believe me."

"Some will."

"It doesn't matter. They'll react to your signals. If you behave as if you're innocent, go on being the best detective in the precinct, this will all fade away. People who aren't your family don't hold on to stuff for long unless there's a reason. If you put it behind you, they'll get caught up in their own dramas. Trust me. It's human nature."

"You trying to tell me the world doesn't revolve around my problems?"

"No. That's your family's job. They'll lord this over you till you die. You might as well just suck it up."

"For a woman with cold fish for parents, you sure do know a lot about large Italian families."

"I'm a quick study. Especially when I'm a little envious."

"Of my family? Whoa. That's hard to get my head around."

"That's because it's all you've ever known. I'd decided long ago that I wanted a big family. A close family. That I would annoy the hell out of my kids and interfere and generally be a pain. I'll make sure they all come to me for the holidays, at least most of them. I'll go to all the recitals and school plays and I'll embarrass my kids in front of their friends." She pressed her face against his chest. "Sorry," she mumbled. "I get carried away."

"That's okay. You'd be good at that. Hell, you'd fit with my people better than I do."

She didn't say anything while she tried to picture it. Nonna's bad cookies. All that Italian macho crap. Dinners with too many people, everyone talking at once. John sitting next to her, holding her hand under the table.

"Bella?"

"Yeah."

"I just wanted to— You know. Uh. I'm still so damn sorry about your audition, but…"

"I know," she said. "Nothing's turned out the way I thought it would today. But only parts of it were really bad."

"Yeah?"

She nodded, stroking his hair again, wishing she could see his dark eyes. "Some parts were pretty great."

His leg wrapped around her tighter. "I was thinking, if you were amenable, that maybe after we're out of here, we could, uh, keep in touch. See each other."

"Well, we already know you're buying me a pair of shoes day after tomorrow."

"Right. Shoes."

"And you should probably take me to dinner. Because, come on. It's the least you could do."

"I see you're gonna lord that over me for the—"

"For the rest of your life? You never know. Stranger things have happened."

He kissed her, and once again it was completely new. There was hope there, and promise.

"It's a damn shame we only had the one condom," he said.

"Huh."

"What?" She could picture his face, how he'd look at her.

"Some detective you are. There's half a box of condoms in that dinky little bathroom."

"Are you serious?"

"I wouldn't joke about that. But then, there are quite a few things I wouldn't joke about."

"Oh, really?"

She scooted down the couch as gracefully as possible considering the cushions had practically swallowed her. "Yep. And I'm going to let you discover each and every one all by yourself."

"Some journeys…" John said, his voice a lot more serious than a moment ago. "Some journeys are meant to be taken slowly. And totally worth each step."

* * * * *

Ms. Step

1

THE OPEN CALL FOR DANCERS wouldn't start for two hours, but Willow Hill's heart raced as if it was only moments away. She'd imagined herself there at least a hundred times, visualizing her perfect posture, the turn of her head when she landed a grand jeté. She could practically smell the powder, the sweat and the competition as every dancer in New York vied for a spot in the best musical since *A Chorus Line*.

Only the few, the proud, the unbelievably good would make the cut. She would be first in line.

Buried in her big blue coat, her tote slung over her shoulder and her eyes peeled for the next free cab, Willow inelegantly stretched her left foot despite her thick boot. At the eight count, she eased the stretch just as slowly. Before she could start on her right foot, she threw her free arm out to catch an oncoming Yellow Cab. Because this was her lucky day, the turning point in her life that would set the stage for the career of her dreams, the cab pulled up to the curb. The driver had enough sense and courtesy to avoid the worst of the puddle and stop a few feet ahead. That didn't happen often, at least not during rush hour. She hurried to the door, adjusted her tote and with one foot still on the curb reached for the handle. Before she made contact, something big and hard slammed into her side.

She fell in slow motion, with vivid snapshots of yellow and black and a long scream that echoed in her head. With a bone-shaking thud she found herself in the gutter, in the black sludge of old snow and grime.

"Damn. Are you all right?"

The deep voice was close above her, concerned, but she couldn't answer with no breath and no equilibrium. A hand touched her arm, another slipped under her head.

"Can you hear me? Are you hurt?"

She inhaled deeply, coughed, breathed again. "I'm fine." She wanted him to let go, give her room. The cab was still there, but if she didn't hurry someone else would grab it.

"Wait, don't," he said.

"Don't what?" Willow found a handhold near the tire and pushed up.

"Move. Don't move."

"It's fine. I'm fine." She shoved him with her elbow. "Go away."

"Not until I know you're okay."

Able to turn at last, she looked up into worried hazel eyes. "What do you want, a letter from my doctor?"

"That would be good, yes."

"Tough. Now either help me up or get lost."

He studied her, his brow furrowed and lips tight. "Let me do the lifting, all right?"

"If it will get you off me."

Carefully, he helped her to a sitting position on the curb, her butt slipping in the slush until he steadied her. Then he ran his hand over the side of her head where she'd hit.

"Hey!" She jerked away. "Bad touch."

"Doctor touch," he said, not letting her escape.

"Not likely."

"True, nonetheless. So be quiet and sit still until I'm sure you haven't split your skull."

She huffed a sigh and gave him two seconds to finish groping her.

"All right," he said. "Let's get you to your feet."

"Finally."

Two sturdy hands lifted her with surprising ease. She meant to step clear of him, be done with this, but pain stole her breath and her balance. Her ankle gave out, and he caught her before she fell.

"What is it?"

"Ankle. Ow. Dammit. Ow." She looked for a place to sit, but there wasn't so much as a decent stoop around. "Open the door."

"What door?"

She looked at the doctor, if he even was a doctor, sharply. "The taxi."

"Oh, yes."

His hands still held her up as she hopped on one foot. This seemed to perplex him, and he looked from the cab door to her and back again. As she opened her mouth to tell him that it wasn't rocket science, the man slung her arm around his neck and picked her up.

"Whoa, whoa. What are you doing?"

"What you asked," he said, as if she were the idiot.

"Who the hell are you?"

"Not Superman. Let's get you in there. I need to look at your ankle."

Willow was surprised at how quickly he managed it. Even more surprised that he scooted in right behind her and immediately bent down to lift her foot.

"Ow!" She flinched and socked him in the arm. Not that he paid any attention. After a soft "Sorry," he had her leg up to his knee, forcing her to lean back against the far door, and was attempting to take off her boot.

It hurt. A lot. "Ow, ow, ow."

He stopped. "This isn't going to work."

"I told you, there's no problem. I stepped wrong, that's all. It'll be fine in a few minutes."

"I doubt it." He turned to the cabbie. "5141 Broadway."

The doctor held her calf in the palm of his hand. It was an awkward position for her, and though she knew he couldn't see up her dress, she felt exposed. Maybe that had something to do with the fact that he was a stranger taking her somewhere unknown. A very handsome stranger, but then Ted Bundy was supposedly good-looking. "I'm not going anywhere with you."

"You need to get to the hospital."

"For a turned ankle? Are you nuts? I've got an audition."

"Audition? For what?"

"A Broadway show, that's what."

His eyes widened a bit before he shook his head. "Unless the part is for someone in a cast, that's not going to happen."

"Cast? No." She vehemently shook her head, her heart plunging to the pit of her stomach. He didn't understand. She had to dance today. She'd come clear across the country, sacrificed everything for this opportunity. The taxi inched into traffic. "Stop." She tried to sit up straight, which was a terrible error. "My bag. It's still out there."

The doctor immediately banged on the partition and the cab stopped. "One minute," he said to the driver. His attention came back to her as he opened his door, carefully placed her foot on the seat, then slipped outside.

Before she had a chance to move, he was back, her tote in hand. Once again he did the ankle-in-his-palm thing before closing the door. The driver didn't waste a moment shooting into the stream of traffic.

"You okay?" He looked as if he actually cared about her answer.

"No. I'm not." Willow let out a breath. She'd danced through injury before. What dancer didn't? But never anything broken. "What kind of doctor are you?"

It took him several seconds to answer. "Orthopedic surgeon. Fourth-year resident. Dr. Flynn Bradshaw."

She let her head fall back against the cab window. "Crap."

"It might not be broken. Although, I don't think you should count on dancing anytime soon."

"This was supposed to be my big break." Tears stung her eyes. She blinked, trying to keep them from seeping. "And not the kind that leaves me crippled. Oh, man. I was sure it was my lucky day. The start of a whole new chapter in my life."

His free hand touched hers. "I'm sorry. Truly."

"It's not your fault." The silence that followed made her stomach clench. "Or is it?"

THE JIG WAS UP. He had to confess, let her know that it was his impatience that had gotten her into this mess, entirely his fault. Luckily, the cab wasn't far from the E.R. entrance, and he was able to deflect for a moment by getting out his wallet. But he could feel her stare.

Flynn ended up giving the driver a ten-dollar tip. It didn't make him feel better. He extracted himself from the backseat and found a wheelchair just inside the hospital entrance. When he got back to the car, her lips were pressed thin. Her watery eyes, a very pretty blue, signaled the end of his grace period. He had to tell her.

She didn't even squeak when he picked her up and

put her in the chair. She just turned her head so she could glare at him.

"I did it," he said. "Not intentionally. I was in a rush, on my cell phone, and I didn't see you and I lunged for the door and crashed into you, and I apologize. I should have been more careful. Watched what I was doing."

She didn't say anything. Not for the whole ride inside. He stood by her as she gave the admitting nurse her information, only then realizing that he hadn't even asked her name. Guilt made him want to pass her on to the attending staff, but when she said she had no insurance, there was no other option. "I'll be taking care of this."

The nurse looked up in surprise. "Dr. Bradshaw? I thought you were going skiing in Vermont."

He shook his head. "Just put my name down as the responsible party."

The nurse, whom he didn't know well, raised her eyebrows, then went back to the paperwork. He didn't dare look at Ms. Hill.

His new patient didn't acknowledge the exchange at all. Her hands gripped the arms of the wheelchair tightly and her cheeks flushed. No way she would forgive him, and why should she? He'd been so looking forward to his ski trip that everything else had disappeared. It felt as if he hadn't had a vacation in years, and God knew he needed one. But first, he'd take care of Willow Hill, which meant his plans would change. He'd been on his way to the ski shop to get a new jacket and goggles, plenty of time to catch his six o'clock flight. He'd planned on ringing in the New Year at a lodge filled with young carefree revelers looking for a good time.

"Dr. Bradshaw?"

He brought his attention back to Ms. Hill. "Yes?"

"You don't have to stay with me," she said, her icy

voice chilling him quite nicely. "Really. Leaving your credit card will be just fine."

He looked at the nurse. "Where can I take her?"

"Seven's open."

"Thank you." He turned the wheelchair and headed down the corridor, past the waiting room, which was, as always, filled to bursting. Tomorrow, he knew, would be even worse. New Year's meant lots of accidents, lots of alcohol poisoning and, for some reason, a lot of babies being born ahead of schedule.

Ms. Hill wasn't any more conciliatory once they were in Exam Seven. He had no idea what would soothe her, and hoped like hell she wasn't thinking lawsuit. For now, all he could do was give her the best the hospital had to offer, including his services.

He helped her up and out of her big down coat, revealing a very slinky black dress covering a very beautiful body. Willow had more curves than he'd assumed. He didn't know many dancers personally, but he treated a lot of them for foot, ankle and knee injuries. They were all ridiculously thin. In Willow's case, she had a small waist, nicely flared hips and a hell of a rack.

After getting her situated on the exam table, he tackled the problem of her boot. "It's going to have to come off," he said.

"Will I need something to bite down on?"

"I'll do my best not to hurt you." He put his own jacket on an empty chair. "Are the boots expensive?"

"Massively. I got them at Tiffany's."

"Oh, that's a shame." He got out the scissors, the big ones they used to cut off clothing, including jackets and shoes.

Her eyes widened at the sight. "I didn't think you were serious. You have to cut them?"

"It's that or risk more damage to your ankle."

A heavy sigh told him she was resigned to her fate. "Do your worst."

Working carefully, he managed to keep his promise. Willow grimaced, but only squealed a couple of times. Her hands clenched tightly at the edges of the table, and she'd closed her eyes. Flynn only glanced at her when he'd put the ruined boot aside. He wasn't sure how to proceed. She'd worn thick tights and he didn't want to destroy those unless he had to.

Pausing for a moment, he looked at her leg, propped up by the tongue of the exam table. Her calves had muscles, but they didn't bulge. He thought she must do yoga or Pilates to get those lean, strong legs.

Her ankle, on the other hand, bulged quite a bit. Even through the material of her tights, he could see she was starting to bruise. "You want to try and take off the tights or should I cut them?"

She winced as she looked at the damage. "Is it broken?"

"We won't know until the X-ray. The ankle is tricky. It could be a sprain, or a torn ligament or tendon. Or it could be broken."

Another sigh. "You'll pay for a new pair of tights?"

He smiled. "Yes."

"I got these at Tiffany's, too."

"I had no idea Tiffany's had such eclectic offerings."

"You have to look in the back room."

"Ah," he said, gently tugging at the tights before he made the first slice.

She hissed through her teeth as he carefully peeled the foot of the tights away.

"We'll get you to radiology in a moment." He put the scissors down.

"When do we get to the painkillers?"

"It aches, huh?"

"Like a son of a bitch."

"We'll make sure you feel no pain. But don't count on anything too heavy-duty."

"You mean I won't get any of the good drugs."

He shook his head although he didn't stop his visual examination. "Probably not. I need to touch a few things first."

"Why?"

"Despite the miracle of X-rays, there are still things doctors need to do by hand."

"Well, be quick about it. I can't believe you did this and you're not even gonna give me good drugs. Some doctor you are."

Flynn caught her eye for a moment and she let him know with a look that she was kidding. Satisfied, he resumed his exam. "So you're an actress?"

"Dancer."

"Been in any shows I might have seen?"

"*Lion King,* maybe. *Rent.* Mostly off Broadway and in reviews."

"It must be exciting."

She hissed again. "I know you're trying to distract me, but maybe we could talk about something other than my now nonexistent career?"

It was his turn to wince. Usually he had a good bed-side manner, at least that's what he'd been told. "Right. You a native?"

"Nope. Californian."

"What part?"

"Bakersfield."

"I don't know it."

"You're not missing much. What about you?"

"Born and raised in Manhattan."

"You don't sound like it."

He put her foot down, got her chart and made some notes. There was a possible fracture in the lateral malleolus, but even if it wasn't broken she was going to be off her feet for a while. "I can talk New York when I need to. Mostly, it was frowned upon."

"By your parents?"

"Yes. Now come on. Let's get you to X-ray. Put your arm around my neck and I'll take your weight."

As she let him help her, her breast pushed against his side and he had to focus on the fact that she was a patient and that he had no business thinking of anything but her ankle. She didn't make it easy, though. Just putting his arm around her waist was an unusual distraction. Maybe because he was already in vacation mode. Whatever, it was inappropriate at the moment.

Finally, she was in the chair looking small and vulnerable. Crap. "Ms. Hill? Willow?"

She looked up at him. Tears again filled her eyes. She blinked and looked away.

Damn. He thought he was immune. Patients cried all the time. "Do you have someone?"

"Excuse me?"

"To take care of you."

She seemed surprised by the question. "Not really. Why? Am I going to need help?"

He wheeled her out the door as he compiled a mental list of who he'd need to call to change his plans. He'd really been looking forward to celebrating tonight. No obligations, no rushing to the hospital in the middle of the night. He would have been free to ski, but more importantly to find a like-minded lady who wanted to party. Instead, he'd have to make sure his new patient was settled and taken care of, which meant he couldn't fly out until tomorrow morning.

"Doc?"

Oh, yeah. The patient. "Yes, I think you will need help. But don't worry. I've got you."

2

FOUR AND A HALF HOURS after the fall, Willow was still trying to digest the fact that while she hadn't broken her ankle, it was still screwed up badly. Very badly. A second-degree sprain. Recovery from four to six weeks. No dancing. No working out. No auditions. To add insult to injury, even then she might require surgery if the ligaments didn't heal properly.

Once more in a taxi, Dr. Bradshaw beside her, they pulled up to her apartment, just a few blocks from Marymount Manhattan College. Thinking about using the crutches to climb the stairs made her feel sick, not that she would admit it. Dammit. She wasn't going to cry again. That's all she'd done since he'd given her the bad news.

He'd tried to make things right. He'd never left her for a minute. He'd not only taken X-rays but also an MRI. Gotten her a coffee and a treat from the nurses' lounge. Put a pillow behind her back. Touched her, rather a lot. Then there was the big one—taking care of the medical costs. But she was grateful to be home. She hated feeling weak. Vulnerable. She'd never liked being fussed over, especially not by the man who'd gotten her into this pitiful position.

"All right." Dr. Bradshaw had gotten out of the cab and held out his arm. "Ready?"

She frowned. "You're not going inside with me. I'll be fine. I can still hobble."

He frowned back. "But you shouldn't. At least not for a few days. You've got injured ligaments and tendons, and you should be lying down."

"I will. I promise."

After a brief shake of his head, which sent a lock of his hair falling across his forehead, he got out of the cab, but not before he told the driver to wait.

"You don't have to stay," she said. "I told you—"

"I'm going to get you inside, and there's not a damn thing you can do about it."

She stared up at him, angry and frustrated. "I'm perfectly capable of taking care of myself. You've done more than enough."

"Please don't argue. I'm tired, and you must be, too."

Okay, he was right about that. She was exhausted. She let him help her out, avoiding the slush at the curb, then slung her arm around his neck. It was already a familiar position. After he'd put her tote over his shoulder, the two of them made it to the stoop, looking as if they were in the world's lamest three-legged race. The ice pack stayed on well as he practically carried her up the two steps and into the small lobby.

Still holding on to her, he swiveled his head to look all around the room. "No elevator?" he finally asked.

"Nope. It's student housing. And ancient."

"What floor are you on?"

She didn't want to tell him. Knowing him, though, he'd follow her up, so there was no use lying. "Sixth."

"What?"

"Sixth. It's the one right above the fifth."

He looked at her as if she'd moved there on purpose. "There's no way you're climbing up six flights of stairs."

"Yes," she said, "there is. That's where I live. All my things are up there."

He shook his head. "This isn't going to work. Don't you have someone who could take you in? Someone who lives on the first floor?"

"Well, excuse me for not having the right friends. I'm not from here, remember? And all the people I know are starving dancers, like me."

"Well, we'll just have to take first things first." Without giving her even a hint of a warning, he swept her up in his arms.

She almost dropped her crutches, and her dress moved up to the top of her thighs. "Hey!"

"Shush." He went to the staircase and began to climb.

Willow couldn't reach her dress unless she dropped the crutches. It was some comfort that she had panties on under her tights, but she still felt terribly exposed. "You can't carry me the whole way."

"Why not?"

"I thought you said you weren't a superhero."

"I'm not. But you don't weigh much and I work out."

"Tell me that again when we reach the sixth floor."

He slowed a bit as he met her gaze. "You really don't think I can do it?"

"I think you'll be the one who needs to lie down."

"How big's your couch?"

She snorted in a very unladylike way. "What couch? I'm sharing a shoebox with three other women. I'm lucky to have a twin bed."

He grinned at her, but he was concentrating on the stairs, not her sparkling wit. There wasn't much else she could do but scope him out. It was impossible to miss how good-looking he was. But on closer inspection she saw there was a ruggedness about him that surprised her.

His light brown hair, longish, thick and with a tendency to lick over his forehead, lured her into thinking he might be too pretty. Then she'd seen the small crescent scar at his right temple and the one on his chin. The capper was his crooked nose. Attractive crooked. Manly crooked. He could have been a street fighter in his younger days. She knew better.

In his attempt to distract her from the end of her life, he'd babbled about his credentials. Yale and med school at Cornell. Smart. Handsome. He must have a wife or a girlfriend. Absolutely no way he was single. Nope, he was taken. For sure.

He turned at the third-floor landing and didn't even hesitate on his way to the fourth.

"You getting tired?"

"Nope."

"Your face says you're lying."

"My face has said nothing at all."

Right. His breathing had changed and while she had to admit he was in wonderful shape, carrying her hundred and four pounds up this many flights would have been hard for anyone. Well, maybe not a fireman, but for the above-average doctor? Oh, yeah.

His steps slowed as they reached the halfway turn on the fourth floor.

"Dr. Bradshaw. Put me down. Please."

He stopped. "What's wrong?"

"I've got a cramp. I'd like to stand up for a minute."

He lowered her feet to the ground, letting her lean against the door and her crutches instead of him. "Where's the cramp?"

"It's nothing," she said, massaging her thigh even though she felt fine. "It's weird being carried. I think I stressed out a little, that's all."

"No problem." He wiped his forehead with the sleeve of his coat.

"You know, you could take that off and let me carry it."

He didn't hesitate. "Good idea. It's warm in here."

"Guess you don't have to go to the gym today." She took his jacket, then remembered. "Your ski trip."

"What about it?"

"You're missing it."

He shook his head. "Another time."

"What?" She put her bad foot down and winced. "It's off? Because of me?"

"Because of my own stupidity."

"No, no. Not gonna happen. Can you still make your flight?"

"It's all right. Maybe I can still catch a plane tomorrow."

"Dr. Bradshaw—"

"Flynn."

"Fine. Flynn. Are you insane? It's New Year's Eve. What about your wife? Or your girlfriend? Someone's going to be pissed. Even the nurse knew you had reservations. I appreciate all you've done, especially the medical costs because I'm broke and that would have been really tricky, but seriously. It's enough. I'm strong. I'm a dancer. Injuries are part of the game. You go on, get out of here."

He stared at her for a long moment. She'd thought his eyes were hazel, but now she saw they were green.

"Your cramp better?"

It took her a second to nod.

"Good. Then let's get you upstairs."

"You're not going to leave, are you?" she said flatly.

He moved closer to her. Definitely green eyes. And he smelled good even though she knew he'd been sweating. He put her arm around his neck and up she went into the cradle of his arms. Against that nice, solid chest. She wouldn't press him further until he'd gotten her inside, but then she was going to insist he leave.

As he continued up the never-ending staircase, she thought about the party she was going to miss tonight. It was at Tommy and Jenny's loft, and they always threw a hell of a bash.

She'd better come up with some reason she'd missed the audition and was going to skip the party. She couldn't tell her friends the truth, especially not Tommy and Jenny. If they knew she'd been hurt pure guilt would have them dropping everything to take care of her, which would have been unbearable. They were great, good buds, but man, longer than an hour with the two of them made her break out in hives. It sure would have been nice to have a boyfriend about now. A real one who stayed longer than a weekend. Someone who'd fetch and carry and worry, but not smother her. She'd have to settle for her roommates' help, even though they were never home.

She rested her head against Flynn's neck as he trudged up the final flight of stairs. God, he smelled good.

FLYNN PUT WILLOW DOWN, letting her balance on her crutches before he inserted her key into the door. Thank goodness it was only six floors. A couple more might have seriously dented his ego. He pushed open the door and froze at what he beheld. The small room was as overstuffed as his Aunt Theresa's ancient couch.

Two big chairs, a twin bed, a television, a stereo and three different coffee tables, each piled higher than the last, left only tiny paths between furniture. Every surface was covered in books and/or clothes, cups and plates. Something furry shifted on one of the chairs, either a big cat or small dog.

"I know," Willow said, her voice still stuffy from all the crying at the hospital. "So stereotypical. But no one's ever here, so it's not quite as disgusting as you'd think."

He turned to her, forcing himself not to shake his head as his father would have. It was a gesture that could make people crazy and he needed her compliant. "This is a problem."

"What is?"

"There's not enough space for you and the crutches."

"I don't stay in this room much. I have a room in the back."

"That's good, but do you also have a kitchen and bathroom in the back?"

"Not exactly."

"Then it's a problem."

She pressed her lips together and gave him a stern look. "I'll deal. Go catch your plane or whatever. Just go."

The solution was obvious, but he didn't blurt it out, especially after that rather unsubtle verbal shove out the door. "Let's get you back to your room."

He took his coat from her and stood aside, wanting to see how she managed. She certainly looked determined. Squaring herself on her crutches she struck out, but only made it past the first of the chairs before she stopped. She'd have to turn sideways to make it through, and it was hard enough to maneuver new crutches without an obstacle course.

Not that he was going to make her try. She'd probably fall and hurt the other ankle. Tossing his coat and her tote on a pile of books, he took the long way around until he faced her again. "Come on, Willow. Let me—"

"No. I can do this."

"But you don't have to."

"What, you're going to stay here and carry me for four to six weeks?"

"No, I've got a better idea. You're going to stay with me."

3

WILLOW REACTED PRETTY MUCH as he'd expected. He'd known she would argue. She didn't know him and certainly didn't trust him. The question, then, was how to prove he wasn't someone to be frightened of.

"You're out of your mind," she said finally. He had no doubt she would have backed away, thrown him bodily out on his ass if she could've. But he had her at his mercy.

Only one thing to do. He pulled out his cell phone, clicked on his contacts and held it out to her. "Call anyone. From any list. I'd go for the hospital first, because there's less of a reason for anyone to lie. Tell them you need to know if you can trust me."

"What?"

"Seriously. Call my boss, Dr. Jefferson. Ask to speak to nurses. They'll be honest. And if you don't want to use my numbers, if you think this is all some evil plot, use your own phone."

She stared at him as if he were crazy. He didn't blame her one iota.

"I suppose it would be less weird if I took you to my sister's. But she's gone and so is her staff. So that wouldn't be any better than you staying in my guest room."

"I need to sit down."

He had to give it to her—she was being very calm

about this. Hopefully, she'd end up seeing his logic. If not, well, he had to try, right? He owed her.

He held out his other hand for her crutches. It took a bit of maneuvering, but finally she had his phone, he had her, and they were inching their way to her bedroom.

Which turned out to be nothing more than a closet with a bed stuffed inside. Along with her clothes, a sort-of dresser, books and lots of dance posters on the wall.

After helping her off with her coat, she sat on the neatly made bed, her gaze on his, clearly befuddled.

"Make some calls," he said. "I want to check on your ankle. How's your pain level?"

"It hurts, but nothing I can't handle."

After a quick check of his watch, he saw he could give her another pill in an hour. He went to one knee and carefully lifted her leg. He undid the Velcro straps holding the ice pack on and put it aside. The swelling hadn't gotten significantly worse. It would be better when she could keep the ankle elevated.

"Yeah, Dr. Jefferson, please. I'm calling about Dr. Bradshaw."

He didn't look up, but he did smile. Good for her. If he had any chance of this working, she had to feel comfortable. As he put her ice pack back on, it occurred to him that he probably wouldn't be able to hire a nurse until after the holiday, and his housekeeper was on her own vacation in Wisconsin checking out her new grandson.

"Hi. This is weird, but I need to know if you'd trust your twenty-four-year-old daughter to stay with Dr. Bradshaw."

Now he looked up. What had he unleashed? He could just picture Jefferson's face. He was a crusty old bastard, but an honest one. He'd been more of a mentor than anyone else at the hospital, but that didn't mean he was going to tolerate this odd line of questioning.

"Right, but say you did. It's a hypothetical question." Willow paused. Rolled her eyes. "Sure. Hold on." She held the phone out. "He wants to speak to you."

Flynn took the phone as he stood. "She's hurt," he said with no preamble. "My fault. She can't stay at her home. I'll look after her at my place. Tell her she'll be safe. Or not." Then he gave her back the phone.

She put it to her ear and after about thirty seconds, she smiled. "Thanks." After she hung up, she clicked down his list of contacts until she found something she liked.

Flynn heard the ring, but not the voice that followed.

"Orthopedic surgery nursing station, please."

He tried to think who would be on duty. With the holiday, there was no way to be sure. They hadn't gone past that station earlier today, so it was a real crap shoot. He tried not to be an ass with the nursing staff, with any staff, but he didn't always succeed.

"Hello," Willow said. "I know you're swamped, but Dr. Bradshaw has offered me a place to stay for a few days when he gets back from vacation. While he's not around, I figured I'd call someone in the know who would tell me if this is a good idea or not."

Flynn wanted to take his phone back. Move closer so he could hear. This was worse than a peer review. Which was crazy.

And then it hit him. What he was doing. He didn't know this woman and except for his guilt he had every reason to leave her to her own devices. He didn't even believe in guilt. Not to this extent, at least. What's done was done, and he'd made his apologies along with financial restitution. Anything more was excessive. Taking a stranger into his home? Caring for her on his only vacation in more than a year? What the hell was he thinking?

Was it because she was attractive? No. He saw attractive women all the time and he only occasionally invited them home, never to stay long. But he had to admit there was something about her. She had guts and determination, no self-pity there. Sure, there had been tears, who could blame her? Instead of using them to play on his guilt and milk the situation, she'd put up a brave front. Maybe not a front at all.

"Really?" Willow said, her eyes widening as she gave him the once-over. "Is he like that all the time?"

He rubbed his hand across his face, his mind dueling the pros and cons of simply taking the phone back and ending this here and now.

"Do the rest of the team think that?"

Think what? That he was a jerk? That he was a decent guy who needed to lighten up? That's what his sister told him. Repeatedly. Easy for her to say, tucked safely away in the suburbs, raising her kids, doing her charity work. She didn't have a career haunted by the Bradshaw name.

"Okay, well, thank you. You've been very helpful. I'll let you know." She hung up the phone, not giving him any clue to the conversation. All she did was stare at him.

He broke first. "Well?"

"So it seems you're civilized enough. She didn't seem to think you were a mass murderer or anything."

"Who did you speak to?"

"Sorry. I promised not to say."

He wanted to press her. "Is that all? That I'm not a serial killer?"

"No. She said more."

He couldn't hold back. He stepped closer. She didn't flinch, so that was something. "And?"

"And I guess I should pack."

WILLOW FELT BETTER THAN she had since the accident. The power had shifted, giving her strength where there had been only vulnerability. If she could keep that look on his face for the next however-long, she could triumph. After all, what was life without adversity? Her heroes wouldn't let a small thing like a screwed-up ankle get in the way of their dreams, right? So she'd stay in the doctor's guest room for a couple of days. Make him fetch things for her. Of course, that wouldn't come close to making up for weeks of missed classes or any chance of an actual dancing gig.

Before she could stop it, her eyes welled with tears again. She wished she was alone so she could cry and scream and beat up her pillows. She didn't have much money, and there's no way she'd be able to keep her cocktail job at the nightclub or get disability. Her savings were supposed to keep her in New York until she hit the big time, but six weeks of no income would eat most of it up. How long would it take to heal and then get back in shape?

"Willow? You okay?"

She felt her lower lip quiver and willed it to stop. "Sure. Yeah. Why wouldn't I be?"

He sat next to her on the bed, close, but not touching. "I can see that's not true."

She pressed her palms to her eyes. Sniffed. Told herself to suck it up.

"I'll make sure you have physical therapy. That you get back to dancing as quickly as possible."

She looked at him, then realized he wasn't telepathic, just paying attention. Kind of nice. "It's a bit overwhelming."

"Not a bit. A lot. I've really screwed up your life."

"It's not as if you did it on purpose."

He didn't say anything. Just sat there looking guilty.

It wouldn't do either of them any good to keep this up. He could have just gotten in the cab this morning and driven away, and there wouldn't have been a thing she could have done about it. She needed to remember that. This could have been so much worse.

"Where do we start?" he asked finally.

Willow pointed to a cupboard above the dresser. "Duffel in there."

He turned to grab it, and she focused on one thing she knew was true. She was her own hero. She would believe that with her whole heart, despite all the evidence. She could get through this. Her parents hadn't believed she could make it in New York, but she'd proved them wrong. So far, at least. And now she had Flynn's help, as well.

Talking to the nurse had actually made her feel a lot better. The woman had three kids, no husband and worked ungodly hours. She'd told her that Dr. Bradshaw was one of the good guys, with only an occasional slip. Then she'd laughed. A real laugh, full of piss and vinegar. Then she'd explained that if she'd known Dr. Bradshaw was so generous with his guest rooms, she'd have signed up long ago.

If Nurse Ellen could laugh at life's twists and turns, then so could Willow. Torn ligaments and lost auditions were nothing in the face of true grit. Or even guilty doctors.

He held up the duffel bag. She smiled. "I'll need all of it."

He didn't even blink. Just got right to work, putting

the bag next to her on the bed. Then he pulled out the top drawer, the only drawer. The rest of it was shelves with folded clothes on top. He proceeded to take all her underwear and stuff it into her bag.

He packed efficiently and without comment. Probably still wondering about the mystery nurse. Maybe later she'd tell him who it was, but then again, maybe not. She'd wait to see how it all worked out. If it was hellish, she could leave. Or he could kick her out. But she doubted she'd have to be on her own before tomorrow.

"Anything else?"

She looked around, amazed at how much he'd crammed into the duffel. Even more amazed at how few things she owned. "Bathroom stuff," she said. "But I'll do that. It's too small for both of us."

"Tell you what. I'll carry you and your crutches in there and leave you to it while I take the bag to the taxi. If he's still there. If not, I'll call another. That should give you plenty of time to get your things together and take care of any phone calls you need to make. Sound like a plan?"

"A great one," she said.

"Will you need another suitcase?"

"Nope. Just my tote."

"All right, then." He bent at the knees until he was at eye level. "It's going to be fine," he said, his voice low and sure. "I promise you don't need to be frightened."

She touched his cheek with the back of her finger. "Neither do you."

FLYNN WAS SCARED TO DEATH.

They'd reached his brownstone. There was no turning back. He felt like an idiot asking a stranger to

his home. Pasting a smile on his face, he left his front
door ajar as he helped her from the cab. Seeing her so
pretty with her cheeks flushed with cold made him even
more uncomfortable. He would have liked to have met
her in Vermont. She was a vacation kind of pretty. The
kind where it didn't really matter what was beneath the
surface because there were only a couple of days to
play. Four to six weeks was a completely different kettle
of fish.

"Would you like to lean on me?" he asked. "Or try
the crutches?"

"Crutches," she said with a nod. "I just haven't figured out this curb business yet."

"Okay, that's easy enough to fix." He crouched, put
his hands around her waist, then looked up to make sure
she wasn't going to smash her head on the door, but he
stalled at her eyes.

They were blue and curious and more scared than her
smile wanted him to know. That made him feel a lot
better. For several reasons. Only one of them was noble.

4

HE HAD A FOYER. No one she knew in New York had a foyer. Especially one with a marble floor and a round table with a huge vase of fresh flowers.

Willow looked at him again, suspicious now that this wasn't his house at all. "Do you live with your parents?"

He laughed. "No. Why?"

"That's a lot of flowers."

The doctor appeared flustered. "I didn't decorate the place."

"Ah. Wife? Girlfriend?"

"Decorator," he said, flustered again.

"Where were you when it happened?"

"Medical school. You need to put your leg up."

She bit down on a smile. "I think I need a tour first. I mean, I am going to be staying here for several weeks."

His face told her she might have gone too far on that one. But he looked good when he blushed.

"You can look around on the way to the guest room."

"Spoilsport."

He carried her bags as she practiced walking with her crutches into the house proper. The foyer didn't do it justice.

This was one of those Manhattan homes that appeared in magazines Willow never bought. Artwork graced the walls, and she, who had gotten a B- in humanities, recognized that it was Serious Art, despite the fact that she could identify the subjects. If memory served, he leaned toward the Impressionists.

The furniture was also Serious. Not as sedate as the marble had suggested, but none of it seemed to fit him. Or maybe she had him figured all wrong.

"Watch the carpet."

She stopped to look down. Sure enough, she'd almost hobbled into an epic fall. "Thanks."

He nodded curtly. Someone in radiology had told her he was one of their better orthopedic surgeons. From everything she'd heard about surgeons, he should have been full of himself and basically a jerk, and yet, here she was.

"It's this way," he said, nodding at a hallway. She carefully made her way past two wing chairs and a fireplace, more paintings and a whole wall filled with hardcover books. The hall led past the kitchen, which was twice the size of her apartment and fully decked out with copper pots and a row of living herbs at a bay window behind the sink.

She wanted to ask him a hundred questions, but he was already standing at the door of what had to be the guest room. Questions would wait. The need to sit was getting more urgent. Her ankle had awakened, no longer appeased by the ice pack.

He led her into the room, which, holy crap, was gorgeous. And come on, a king-size bed? This had to have been his grandparents' house. No one in his early thirties lived like this.

Maybe he was older than she thought. She watched as he bent to put her stuff down. He sure had the ass of an early thirties guy. At least with clothes on.

"So, did your decorator come here right after doing Windsor Palace or what?"

"I thought it might please you, Your Majesty."

"Hey. I see what you did there." She hopped over to the bed and sat on the incredibly expensive-looking spread. "Clever."

"Stop ragging me about it. I was in school. It's all family stuff, that's all."

"Some family."

"Yeah." Flynn glanced at his watch, then at her.

Willow hadn't missed the sarcasm packed into that one word, no matter how subtle. So the life of the rich wasn't so perfect.

"Where did I put your pills?"

"Tote."

"Right." He picked up the bag and brought it to the bed. "First, let's get you prone."

"Ooh. That sounds interesting."

He stopped. Dead. She blushed and wished she was one of those witty women who could turn a quick phrase. But she wasn't. She was a hopeful dancer from Bakersfield who hadn't learned to think before she spoke.

After clearing his throat, Flynn fluffed some pillows at the head of the bed. "Get settled. I'll bring you some water. I'm sure you can find the pills in your bag."

"You bet." She tried to smile as if she'd never suggested they should sleep together. "Absolutely. No problem."

His forehead furrowed and there might have been a tiny tic at the edge of his right eye, but she couldn't be sure because he left. Her gaze swept down his back as he did so, and while she tried to convince herself that the remark had been nothing more than a slip of the tongue, in her heart she knew a Freudian slip when she heard one.

CRAP.

Flynn cursed himself for being such an obvious twit. She had to know he found her attractive. More than just attractive. But she was still his patient, dammit. That technicality hadn't mattered to his father, but it did to him. Mattered all the more because his arrogant father had flaunted his mistresses. Not that anyone had talked about it. Calvin Bradshaw had been far too important and wealthy to be called to the carpet. But everyone knew. And everyone assumed like father, like son.

Hell, everything would have been fine if Flynn hadn't run into Willow. He'd have felt no remorse at hooking up with someone in Vermont. He'd even bought a new box of vacation condoms. He'd had every intention of using them all up, too, and now…

He turned on the kitchen light and went to the fridge. Once opened, he remembered that he hadn't stocked up on anything. There were a couple of bottles of water, some bacon, no eggs. Apples that had been there a long time. He shifted the mayonnaise jar, but nothing great was lurking behind it.

He'd have to shop. He hated shopping. And it would be crowded everywhere because of the holiday.

He cursed. Loudly. Then he took a deep breath, got a bottle of water and headed back to the guest room. Halfway there, he turned around, went back to the kitchen for a notepad and this time he made it all the way.

She had gotten herself comfy with her back against the pillows, but adjustments needed to be made. He opened the cap on the water bottle before he handed it to her, then he went to the closet and brought out a pillow and a comforter.

When he turned, she was still downing her pills. She

hadn't taken off her tights, but she had removed her other boot. Her dress had been tugged down demurely, but he remembered too well the sight of her in his arms on the steps leading to her apartment. The way her hem had come all the way to the top of her thighs, teasing him with what was still hidden. Had she known his breathing had changed because of that and not exertion?

"Here," he said, spreading the comforter over her legs. "Let's get that ankle elevated." He flipped back the cover so only the bottom of one leg was bared. "And I need to change your ice pack."

"I can do that."

"No, you just relax. There's a TV in that armoire. It's got cable. I have lots of books and I'm sure I can pick up any I don't have in my library." He took off the ice pack and put the pillow under her foot. The swelling looked about the same, thanks to the ice, but tomorrow the ankle would really blossom. "I don't have anything to eat in the house, so I'm going shopping. What can I pick up for you?"

She put the water bottle on the bedside table and didn't look back at him for a while. "I don't need much. Mac and cheese would be good. You know, the blue box? And maybe some noodle soup?"

"I guess you weren't kidding about being a starving student. We can do better than that."

She pulled the comforter up over her waist. "Actually, those are the opposite of foods I regularly eat. Being a dancer means mostly I eat vegetables. Fish. Some fruit. Basically, nothing fun."

"Mac and cheese is fun?"

"It's comforting."

He sat down on the edge of the bed, not wanting to disturb her leg, but this was better. Willow was more relaxed, which meant he could relax. At least for now. "You sure you want the blue box, huh? There's a restaurant a couple blocks from here that makes great noodles. I think I have a menu in the kitchen. And they deliver."

"Sounds wonderful."

He handed her the notepad and pen. "Write down everything you want. I mean it. I have nothing here. Soda, tea, coffee, milk, whatever. You might as well get what you like. I'm going to get another ice bag."

She nodded. As he walked away, he wondered if it was a good idea to leave so soon. The nervous energy was leaving her and she was going to crash. He'd seen enough patients to know the pattern, and letting her sleep uninterrupted would be the best thing for her. But he didn't know Willow. Maybe she'd get frightened, or be too upset to conk out. His instincts leaned toward letting her be while he shopped. He'd give her his cell number and make sure she knew she could call him.

Once back in the kitchen he traded ice packs, then stopped to check his voice mail. Of course Andy had called. Flynn dialed him as he put together a pot of coffee. He wasn't going to turn the thing on until he was back from shopping and by then he'd have milk.

"Where the hell are you?" His old college buddy and fellow resident was as direct as ever.

"Take three guesses."

Andy gave him the usual lecture about needing breaks and not being such a sap.

"It's complicated. Anyway, it means less competition for you."

And then came the Overachievers Burn Out Young Speech. Eventually, things got quieter on the phone and Flynn gave his friend the digest version of his day. Of course, that led to many, many sound reasons he was insane for asking a stranger into his home, and a chick at that.

"It was my fault. She can't work for weeks. What was I supposed to do, have the cab slow down near the hospital and shove her out the back door?"

"You're paying her medical expenses. Jeez, what else could she hope for?"

"An attorney could think of quite a few things, I'd imagine."

Andy sighed. "Is she hot at least?"

"She's a patient."

"So? Is she?"

It was Flynn's turn to sigh. "Yes, dammit, she is hot. But she can't do anything but keep her leg on a pillow. She's hurt. Nothing's going to happen."

"My man, it's New Year's Eve. I don't care if she's in a complete body cast, if you can't get some tonight, you're out of the club. Forever."

"I was never in the club."

"And this," Andy said, "is why."

"Go find a cold woman with a dark heart and leave me my dignity."

"Dignity be damned, man. You haven't been laid in months."

"Thanks for announcing that to the mountain."

"I'm in the lodge. Hold on."

Flynn heard more chatter as Andy did something with the phone. Then, from a slight distance, "I'm talking to Flynn Bradshaw, M.D. He hasn't been laid in months. Just so y'all know."

Andy came back on, and Flynn could practically see

his gloating grin. "Okay, then. My work is done. The woman is hot, you fool. Don't screw it up."

A click, and it was just Flynn and an ice pack and a hot stranger in his guest room.

5

WILLOW WISHED SHE'D CHANGED clothes before getting on the bed. Tiredness had swooped in like a wraith and stolen not only her energy, but her swagger, leaving her feeling awkward as hell.

She clearly hadn't thought things through.

The notepad was still empty. Charity, it turned out, didn't fit well. She didn't mind him paying for the medical things, but him buying her food? Him actually nursing her? Him in general? Too much. Too scary. Too intimate.

There wasn't really any *fear* fear. The scary part was that she was in his home, in his bed. Not where he slept, sure, but he did own the actual bed. Okay, that wasn't the scary part. Uncomfortable, yes, but not technically scary. The scary was that she liked him.

He was nice. And he'd cancelled his vacation. In spite of his excellent ass and being handsome, he was more than a decent guy. He was pretty terrific.

She wasn't used to more than decent. In her experience, the guys she liked the best tended to be gay. The men she dated—Greg, for example—hadn't been stellar. High school had been filled with a series of popular kids as she'd been more concerned with fitting in than fitting well. College had been Matt, the sax player. He'd been okay, just not very attentive unless sex was on the menu. Then came New York and actors. Whoa, talk about a learning curve. Turns out she wasn't a great sycophant. Who knew? So the auditions, the classes, the occasional hookup with a friend of a friend. The major lesson being that she needed to take care of herself.

Then this. Him. It was disorienting, to say the least.

He walked into the room carrying another ice pack. He seemed kind of dazed.

"Flynn?"

He sat down at the foot of the bed. "Yeah?"

"This is weird."

"What?"

"Being here. I can tell you're as uncomfortable as I am. We need to rethink this."

"I'm not uncomfortable," he said as he avoided her gaze. "I'm sorry you are."

"Want to try that again?"

"Okay, it's different." He flipped back the comforter and pointedly looked at her ankle. "I don't see an alternative, at least for now."

"I can go home."

"Nope. However weird this feels, it will be a lot worse if I let you do that."

"Noble, but unnecessary. I'll make do."

He put the ice pack back, circling her ankle, Velcro-strapping it in place. His hands were cold, but he was careful, gentle. When he put her foot down on the pillow, his palm brushed over her foot before he covered her leg. The gesture was sweet. Almost like a kiss to make it better.

He met her gaze this time, his face more relaxed. "Let's see how we feel tomorrow. For tonight, just think of this as a hotel room. Fill out your meal request and I'll get you the remote for the TV. Sleep. Heal. Bring in the New Year as well rested as possible. That's what I plan to do."

"One night. Then we regroup."

"Yep."

She could do that. "Then do me a favor." She held out the pad and paper. "I don't care what you get. I'll eat almost anything. Just no eggplant. Or cilantro."

His laugh sounded great, all relaxed and easy. "Nothing special?"

"Does this store have a bakery?"

"No, but the bakery next door to it does."

Her own smile was easy, too. Tired, though. "If that bakery had a chocolate éclair, that would be amazingly great."

"Ah. Pastry. Good choice."

"Not just any pastry." She held out her hand. Flynn took it, and she pulled herself forward so she could fix the pillow behind her head. When it felt right, she let go of him.

He didn't let go of her.

"What?" she asked, not at all sure how to read his current expression.

"You don't want to sleep in your dress."

Eyes widening, all she could think to say was, "Probably not."

He let go of her hand. "I just meant if you need any help before I leave…"

"Yeah, sure. I mean, if you could bring my duffel bag, I could get out my, you know…"

"Right."

A moment later, the big green bag was on the bed next to her. She turned to grab her nightgown, but it was awkward and she winced as her foot slipped off the pillow.

"Easy." Flynn grabbed her right wrist and eased her back to her sitting position. Then he straightened out her leg and the comforter. "Now, let me help you." He walked around the bed and dove into the duffel bag as if it contained presents.

"Bathroom, right?" He held up her makeup bag and her toothbrush case.

A nod, and he was gone into the connecting room. She hadn't seen inside it before and ducked her head for a look. It was as decked out as the rest of the house. She also realized she needed to get acquainted with the facilities.

He was back in a flash. "What else goes in there?"

"Uh, me."

"We can arrange that."

She grinned at the fact that while he sounded like it was no big deal at all, his darting eyes told the real story. "Just help me on to the crutches. I can take it from there."

He hustled to get her squared away, and she decided she'd consider this pampering—going along with the whole hotel metaphor. He was her Jeeves. She'd always wanted one. As she closed the door behind her, she wondered if he'd be willing to speak with a British accent. Just for tonight, of course.

It took a little more time than she was used to, but she managed to take care of business without breaking any bones or porcelain tchotchkes, of which there were many, including a tissue dispenser, a soap thingie, a dish that held cotton balls and another that held potpourri. Even the sink was porcelain. It reminded her of her grandmother, although thankfully nothing was painted with little hearts and flowers.

A gentle tap on the door almost made her lose her footing, but the counter came to the rescue. "Yes?"

"I have your nightgown here," he said. "I thought you might like to change while I'm still around, just in case."

"Oh, good idea. Hold on." She hopped the two steps to the door and opened it a crack. The nightgown appeared and her hand stilled inches from grabbing it.

It wasn't the nightgown she would have chosen. She had a flannel thing that was old and ugly and had a tear along the hem.

This one was definitely not flannel. It was red. Silk. Short. See-through.

"Is something wrong?"

He sounded innocent. But even he had to know this was a nightgown for sex, not sleeping. It was that damn comment she'd made earlier. That and the way she'd ogled.

The question was, did she mind? She'd gone back and forth so many times today she barely knew which end was up. There was no way she was going to make a sex decision while she was this wiped out.

"Willow?"

"No, nothing's wrong. Did you happen to bring my robe with you?"

"I'll go get it."

Problem solved, at least for the moment.

He was back in a sec with both garments. She ended up doing most of her undressing and dressing from a seated position, but finally she was safely tucked in her robe and ready for sleep.

She opened the door to find the bed turned down, her duffel bag put away, the TV remote next to her water and the foot pillow under the covers. Flynn stood near the armoire looking pleased with himself.

"Nicely played, Dr. Bradshaw."

"The Bradshaw Inn strives to meet all our guests' needs."

She used the crutches to cross to the bed. "Well, that'll have to wait till I get some sleep." Now that she was at the bed, she wasn't sure if she should take off the robe or wait for him to leave.

She turned to look at him, surprised to see him gaping at her. Cheeks flushed, right eyebrow crooked so high it almost met his hairline.

Then it hit her. What she'd said. *Shit.*

Putting on her most casual smile, she said, "You know, I'm good. I've got everything under control here, so hey, you go do what you need to and don't even think about…anything. And, um, could you make that two éclairs? No, three. No, two. Two is enough. More than enough. Two éclairs is a huge amount of…"

"Yeah. Two it is. Get some rest and I'll…"

She turned her back and winced until she heard him close the door. After counting to ten to make sure he'd really gone, she got out of her robe, made it under the covers and nearly wept with the effort it took to get her stupid leg up on the pillow.

All she needed was sleep. Sleep and a time machine. She closed her eyes, knowing she'd never sleep now. Dammit.

FLYNN PUT DOWN the two big bags of groceries he'd picked up at the corner market and took a number from the dispensing machine on the bakery counter. He'd dawdled while shopping, debating his moves upon returning to the house.

On the one hand, Andy was right. It had been a long time since he'd been with a woman. Hell, it had been a long time since he'd been with his good pal Lefty. Work had swallowed him whole, making him a very dull boy, indeed. Which he'd expected. He'd decided on surgery as his career with the full understanding it would mean putting his life on hold. Still, Willow was someone he'd have pursued if he'd had the time, if they'd met under different circumstances. And that scenario could have involved sex as a jumping-off point.

The fact that she was thinking along similar lines was a major plus.

On the other hand, she had a bad sprain, which he'd caused. She'd been exhausted, so nothing she'd said could mean anything, not really.

On the other-other hand, she was hot, she was nice and it was New Year's Eve.

His number was called and he turned to the harried woman behind the counter. "You have éclairs?"

"Yes," she said, and while her voice was steady and almost cheerful, her eyes begged him to hurry and go.

"I'll take a dozen," he said, throwing caution to the wind. "And a loaf of French bread."

The woman went off to box and bag and he laughed at his own stupidity. A dozen? Compensating much? Ah, who cared. It was pastry. He'd already splurged on champagne. Along with milk and eggs and other necessities, he'd picked up some good soft cheese and an assortment of fruit. Even if Willow slept until tomorrow, he'd treat himself to some goodies. This was his holiday, too. He wouldn't miss having sex so much if he was drunk and full.

The woman returned and he paid her in cash. He wished her a happy New Year, then headed back down the street, watching all the other pedestrians hurrying to get home, to get to parties, to get laid, to finish off the year with something that was special, something different. Maybe even to mark a new beginning, as well as a solid farewell.

An arbitrary date on an arbitrary calendar, but people gave it meaning. For him, it was another year of his residency under his belt. Another step taken toward his ultimate goal. No, make that career goal. His ultimate objective was a full, well-rounded life. A healthy marriage. A practice, sure, but one with reasonable hours and time for any kids that might come along. Flynn would be a good surgeon, perhaps even a great one. But not at the cost of his soul.

6

FLYNN LISTENED AT THE guest room door, unsure whether to knock or peek in to check on Willow. She needed to sleep and the siren's call of a nap tugged at him all the harder for thinking of it. He turned the knob and inched open the door until he could see the bed.

Ah, success. She had sacked out, and very prettily at that. Her right hand shared her pillow, curled in a loose fist, next to her jaw. That lovely, honey hair had spread around her peaceful face, and she looked so comfortable he was tempted to join her under the covers.

Instead, he quietly closed the door and returned to the kitchen to put away the groceries. First up was to refrigerate the champagne along with the pastries. He didn't even glance at the coffee, knowing he needed at least an hour of decaffeinated rest. Once everything was in order, he made the trek upstairs to his bedroom. His suitcase was still on the bed, ready for takeoff.

Without removing a single item, he tossed the suitcase on the floor and fell on the mattress like a dead thing. He had a moment to think of the woman downstairs, but only a moment.

IT WAS DARK when she woke. There was a handy clock on the bedside table, which told her it was just past nine.

If she hadn't believed it before, there was no doubt now that she'd lost her chance to be on Broadway.

How long would she be sitting on the sidelines, watching friends and people she really disliked getting gigs that should have been hers? Four to six weeks might sound okay on paper, but in her world that was an eternity. What about work? What about classes? No auditions, no ballet, no jogging in the park. Impossible. She was an athlete, for heaven's sake, and a serious one. Her life revolved around her physical self. She'd never been sidelined like this before, never.

There had been dance classes, gymnastics and jazz and cheerleading. Competitions, awards, rehearsals, practicing when the other kids were sleeping in or playing or having sleepovers. She regretted none of it, but now it was as much a part of her as breathing, and she had no idea who she was if she wasn't a dancer.

All that stuff before about feeling scared? Nothing. *This* was scared.

She looked at the door, at the window, at the clock, and then she closed her eyes and took a deep breath. She'd come to New York without knowing a soul. She'd used all her own money. She'd gotten into shows on talent and persistence. She could get through this. She *could*.

After a lot more deep breaths and a lot of envisioning herself bathed in white light, she opened her eyes again, the panic in her stomach somewhat eased. Not all the way, but then she remembered the only thing she could control was right now. And right now, she had a kink in her neck.

She usually slept on her side, but she'd been afraid to move in case her leg fell off the pillow. She stretched, and that felt so good she stretched some more and that's when the throbbing in her ankle perked up.

It wasn't difficult to reach the bedside lamp. She wondered if Flynn was home yet. She had no idea how long she'd slept as she hadn't looked at the clock before she'd conked out.

She hoped he was home. Despite her mini meditation, it still felt odd as hell to be here. Even when she pretended it was a hotel room. The remote was right there so she turned on the TV and flipped through the channels. Oh, my, he had all the cable stations. Fancy.

There were movies she hadn't seen, *South Park,* ohh, *Buffy.* That settled that. She had watched the series so often she knew exactly what was going on with Spike and Dru. The show was the TV version of eating mac and cheese and she felt her shoulders relax into the pillows.

Still, she kept hitting the mute to listen for him, but there was only silence. No knock, no footsteps. She ought to get up. Do something about her cotton-filled mouth. On her way back to bed, she'd open her door. That way, he would know that she was up. If he was home. If he was awake.

It was once again a real pain to get on her feet. The crutches weren't all that comfy on her pits, and she hated feeling like such a klutz. Shutting the bathroom door had never been a battle before, but she finally won. The brushing of the teeth felt divine. So good, she washed her face with the delicate-smelling soap and brushed her hair to boot.

That's when she realized she hadn't put on her bathrobe. So, did she open the bedroom door first, then go to bed, or get the robe, then the door…

Forget it. If he saw her, he saw her. It was bound to happen if she ended up staying here for days and days. Maybe she even wanted it to happen.

He had such great hands. No rings, and his nails were neat and clean and he smelled good.

Her heart hammered a bit as she opened the bedroom door, prepared to see him standing there, hand up ready to knock. Nope. Just dark hallway. So she slowly turned, careful not to hit anything with her crutches, and started back to bed.

"You're up."

The voice behind her scared her into catching the crutch on the carpet. She panicked, dropping the right crutch so she could brace for the fall, but hands grabbed her waist just before she crashed.

"Shit," he said, pulling her back to upright. "I didn't mean to scare you."

"It's okay. I think." Her panic blossomed as he stepped closer, pressing his body against her back. She couldn't do anything but clutch his arm and try not to put her bad foot down.

"You're all right?"

"Yeah. Fine."

He didn't move. She felt his breath on the curve of her neck, his heat on her bottom and a bit more pressure where his hands held her steady. The nightgown was so slight it was as if he were touching her skin. She stood as still as possible, tummy all aquiver, waiting to see what he would do and hoping not to fall.

"You're, uh…"

"Yes?" Her voice came out whispery. She listened to him breathe.

"I should get you into bed."

Her eyes closed and so did her mouth as she tried not to take that the wrong way.

His hands braced her until he was at her side. Somehow she managed to get her free arm around his neck and he helped her hop to the side of the bed. And yes, her boob rubbed against his chest. From there it was an awkward dance until she was sitting down. His gaze went directly to her nipples, which could probably take an eye out if she weren't careful. Nothing she could do about it, so she used her audition smile. It took him a long time to notice.

Flustered again, he tried to smile back, but it was only somewhat successful. "You hungry?"

"Famished."

"Want food or éclair?"

"You got me some?"

"More than some," he said, taking little steps away from her, his hands shoved in his pockets. He'd changed clothes. Nicely worn jeans with a slate-gray silky shirt. He'd showered. He really was a good-looking man.

"How many more?" she asked, forcing her mind to focus on edibles.

"I got a dozen."

She laughed out loud and he gave her an honest grin.

"What? I panicked."

"In a good way," she said, still unsure of so much, but not really minding.

"I also got champagne."

"Wow."

"I'm not sure you should have any. Although you're only taking NSAIDs."

"I thought I was taking high-dose aspirin."

"You are. NSAID is the technical term."

"Ah. Doctorspeak."

"Anything to confuse the patient, that's my motto."

"Okay, how about I take another one of those NSAIDs and you fix me whatever you're having for dinner."

"Followed by éclairs and champagne?"

"Exactly."

He looked at her breasts again, froze for a moment,

then turned in a hurry. "Right. Couldn't get the mac and cheese because the restaurant had a line halfway down the block, but I only found out after I'd been to the store. Oh, the pills are in the drawer. I hope you like soup and grilled cheese sandwiches, and I'll be back later."

She watched him go all the way down the now-lit hallway before she got the bottle of pills, thinking all the while that for a doctor he was awfully cute. Her thoughts turned to the champagne and dessert portion of the evening, and she popped two pills just in case.

FLYNN SLAMMED THE LIGHT on with his elbow then threw the fridge door open. This was ridiculous. He'd woken up with a hard-on. Fixed that problem with a record-setting jerk-off in the shower. End of discussion. Until he walked into the guest room to find his patient as good as naked.

Which was his own damn fault. He'd seen something flannel in her bag, but he'd gone for the red slinky number. He hated thinking with his dick. At least at home. On vacation he could shut off all cognitive functions and be as decadent as he wanted, which was usually not terribly decadent, but not here. Not with Willow.

He pulled out the cheese and the butter, a Granny Smith apple, some deli ham and mustard and put it all on the counter. Man, she was pretty. Those breasts. He couldn't stop staring at them. The whole hard-on problem? Still a problem. No, he hadn't gotten absurdly rigid, but he'd been well on his way.

What the hell was wrong with him?

As Andy had pointed out to him and the public at large, he hadn't gotten any for a long time. But that didn't mean he wasn't in control. He wasn't seventeen. But man, she was pretty.

To make things worse, he liked her. She'd be fun to get naked with. Playful, for sure. She certainly was full of surprises. He knew without a doubt that if he were in her position, he'd be raising hell. He probably would have contacted a lawyer already. Not that she would. She wasn't the type. But if nothing else, hadn't his father taught him to be prudent? To keep his johnson far away from his patients?

He put the sauté pan on the stove to get hot as he buttered the bread. The recipe was one from his child-hood. Not a typical grilled cheese, but he'd wager she'd like it. She struck him as someone who liked to try new things. Her career choice was proof of her daring.

It didn't take long to assemble the sandwiches and get the soup out of the cupboard. Clam chowder felt right, and he could pop that in the microwave while the cheese melted.

He even had a tray so she could eat in bed.

He wanted to eat with her, next to her. To spend the rest of the evening drinking cold champagne and stuffing himself with high-fat food. It was tiresome, always being so careful. About food, about women, about his residency, about everything.

For one night, couldn't he toss out the rules? Have some fun? Make her feel good?

He stopped, his knife halfway to the mustard crock. Making her feel good had a nice ring to it. After all, he was responsible for turning her life upside down. The least he could do was make her happy.

7

THE SOUND OF HIS FOOTSTEPS in the hallway sent her whole body into hyperdrive. Heart racing, nerves tingling, anticipation off the charts. Which was stupid. She was injured, and she was his guest and no one had said anything about anything really, so she should just cool her jets and calm down. And yet, she touched her hair, cleared her throat and licked her lips, then sighed at her pitiful self.

He appeared at the door carrying a huge tray full of delicious smells. He smiled. She smiled back. Flutters happened.

"Did you take your pill?"

"I did," she said. Five minutes ago she had pushed an extra pillow against the headboard, an invitation for him to join her. Now it seemed too much. "The ankle is behaving itself."

He stepped across the threshold and then stared at the bed for a moment. She could almost see him figure out her impulsive plan. Only she couldn't tell if he thought it was a good idea, a terrible idea or if he had just crossed her off his list forever.

The tray, being so large, was put in the middle of the bed where she saw there were two smaller trays right next to each other. Both had nice bowls of steamy clam chowder and beautifully golden sandwiches. Also two containers of cranberry juice. Two.

He leaned over her to lift one tray, then put it on her lap. He smelled even better than the food. There was a cloth napkin, gold in color, and a soup spoon. Willow felt like a princess. Or at least someone very rich.

"You comfortable?"

She nodded. "This looks fabulous."

"Old family recipe."

"The soup?"

"Uh, no. That was canned. But the sandwich is." He slipped the napkin from underneath the spoon and flapped it open. His pause was adorable. Would he actually put it on her chest?

Deciding it was better to have him relaxed, she took the napkin and did the honors herself.

Flynn seemed relieved as he headed around the bed, glancing at the chair in the corner. But then he simply sat next to her as if it were no big deal and her worries were nonsense. "I figured we could eat together, watch a little TV. If that's okay."

"Sure. That's fine," she said, in her most casual voice. So why was she still nervous and anxious and wondering if her attraction was as real as it felt or just a distraction from the collapse of her life as she knew it? Not that she'd let on. She smiled as if this sort of thing happened to her twice a week.

"You know, I don't think I've ever been on this bed before," he said as he settled his tray on his lap.

"Really? Has anyone?"

He nodded. "My sister and her husband. My nephew. My friend Andy stays here when he's too smashed to get home."

"Does that happen often?"

"From time to time. Only when he's not on call and has a few days off."

Okay, talking was good. Really good. In fact, maybe she'd spend the rest of the meal asking him questions. "Is that what you do when you're not on call?"

He smiled in lieu of an answer.

She took half her sandwich and resisted the urge to peek inside. She wasn't a fussy eater, but some things were a bit exotic for her Bakersfield tastes. The first bite told her not to be concerned. It was scrumptious.

"Really?" he asked.

She nodded, making the yummy sound again.

"I know it's not typical."

"It's much better. Spicy and creamy and crisp and soft all together. And there's something sweet. Apple?"

He gave her a new smile. One that showed more than his excellent dental hygiene. He might be a big important surgeon, but just like little ol' her, he needed the attaboys. "Then you won't mind the canned soup so much."

"You're right. I won't."

He took a big bite himself, then straightened the pillow before he relaxed back, for all the world looking like a man settling down for the duration.

"Is Andy also an orthopedic surgeon?"

"Neurologist."

"Doesn't alcohol kill brain cells?"

"Luckily for him he's got them to spare. The moron's brilliant. He aced every test all through school, completely destroying the bell curve. I have no idea why we're friends."

"Sounds like a healthy competition. I mean, you've had ample opportunity to strangle him in his sleep."

"Ah, the mess afterward. He's very tall. Not worth it."

She ate some more, liking his sense of humor very

much. And also liking the pauses between the Q & A. In fact, they were nice. Easy. Still, she wanted to know so much more about him. "Is Andy enjoying his vacation as we speak?"

"Yes, he is."

"Did he yell at you for staying here and playing nursemaid?"

"He did."

"I think we'd get along, then."

Flynn nodded. "He'd hit on you before you could say hello."

"You mean he doesn't use the knock-'em-senseless technique? It's very good, you know. Although you could have tried just introducing yourself."

Flynn closed his eyes and dropped his chin to his chest.

She patted his hand. "It's okay."

"But it's not. You're a career dancer. I've put you out of work."

"That might be a bit of a stretch."

"Oh?"

"The goal is to be a career dancer. Right now, I'm a sometimes dancer, more often cocktail waitress and student."

"A cocktail waitress?"

"Don't knock it." She sniffed. "The tips pay for that palace I live in."

"How can you be so flip? You realize you can't work for at least four weeks."

She swallowed. "I know."

"Will you still have a job?"

"I hope so."

He shook his head with self-disgust. "What will you do in the meantime?"

"Hang out at Grand Central Station, hop on one leg

and set out a hat. I heard people are particularly generous on Friday afternoons."

"I'm serious."

"Fine. I don't know. I haven't thought that far ahead. Something will work out." Meeting his gaze, she waited until he could look at her calmly. "It was an accident. They happen. And you've more than made up for everything. Please, let the guilt go." God, she was a good actress. Maybe if she convinced him it was no big deal, she'd convince herself. "I'm frustrated about missing the audition, but there are going to be more auditions. Maybe I needed to slow down a bit, and this is the universe's way of helping me."

"You're amazing, you know that?" he said, smiling.

"Shut up. It's the painkillers talking."

Amusement lit his eyes. "Are you really just twenty-four? Or was that another hypothetical you gave Dr. Jefferson?"

"Impertinent."

"I'm a doctor."

"So what?"

He opened his mouth, then shut it quickly. "That line always works."

"Do people give you their ATM pins, too?"

"Hmm. Haven't tried."

She took a spoonful of soup, now that it wasn't so hot. It was good, a perfect companion to the sandwich.

He followed her cue and went back to his dinner. They both stared at the television, which was still muted. *Buffy* had been replaced by reruns of *House*.

"Does this show make you crazy?" she asked.

"Yep."

"But you still watch it?"

"Yep."

"Why?"

He thought for a second. "Catching their mistakes makes me feel smart."

Her hand went back to his, just for a second. "You don't need a medical show to know that."

"No, no, I don't." His eyebrow rose in that way of his. "For that, I need *Jeopardy*."

She laughed, and he looked pleased. The ruggedness she'd noticed before was still there at cross-purposes with his hair, yet somehow it made sense. She hadn't known him long, but she already knew he was a complex man. Not easily categorized. "Why'd you become a surgeon?"

He swallowed his bite, staring at the foot of the bed as he did so. "I originally wanted to be an engineer. When I was a kid, I mean. Make things. Take them apart and build them better. But then at sixteen I broke my leg playing baseball. The doctor was a friend of my father's and he explained the procedure in detail. I realized that the human body is more interesting than any building or piece of machinery."

"Is it still interesting?"

He nodded. "Fascinating."

"So, orthopedics. That's because of the broken leg, too?"

He hesitated. "Sort of."

"Hey, if you don't want to talk, that's okay."

"It's not that…"

Okay, now he'd gotten her curious. "Well?"

"My father is a heart surgeon. A famous one."

"Ah, I see. Hard to follow in his footsteps."

"That's the last thing I want to do." He slid her an exasperated look. "Brilliant surgeon. Lousy husband, lousier father.

"Now, how about you? Did you always want to be a dancer?"

She wanted to keep asking him questions, but she could take a hint. "It's what I've done my whole life. I started dancing school when I was five. Never stopped."

"Because it was what you wanted? Or was there something else going on?"

Okay, interesting. His tone had changed with that last question. He meant did she have a stage mother, but there was more to it than that. There was a subtle urgency in his voice, almost an anger. Was this about his father again? "My mother," she said, "was always proud of me, but she wasn't insistent. She wanted me and my sister to have options. We played sports, swam, joined Girl Scouts, learned musical instruments. Dancing was the one that stuck for me. My sister liked science. She's going to be a biochemist."

"Older or younger?"

"She's older. By one year. She goes to UCLA."

"You miss her?"

"A lot. She helped me with all my math homework."

"Good thing you don't have to worry about that now."

Willow smiled, missing Skye. "She helped with other things, too. Hey, you said you had a sister?"

"I do. She's the mother of two great boys. Married to a doctor, which isn't a shock. She lives in Connecticut with her husband and my mother."

"So I take it your parents are divorced."

"Separated. Going on ten years."

"Well, no use making a hasty decision."

He chuckled. "It's more like why air dirty laundry when everyone can go on pretending we have the perfect family."

"I'm sorry."

He shrugged. "I've made peace with it. I just refuse to be like him. All he cared about was his practice and his mistresses. Not necessarily in that order. He had two separate penthouse apartments where he kept them. Nicely, I might add. Chauffeurs, maids, wardrobes, cosmetic surgery. God forbid one of his babes looked older than twenty."

Yeah, there was still some anger there. "So," she said, blatantly changing the subject, "you're, like, loaded."

He laughed. "Yeah, I suppose we are. Maybe not as loaded as we used to be, but my great-great-grandfather made some fortuitous choices."

"And all this furniture came from his house, I assume?"

He looked at her crossly. "Quit hating on my furniture. It's not that bad."

She gave him a look right back. "If you're ninety."

"Okay, okay. I know. And when I finish my fellowship, I promise I'll buy all new things. Cross my heart."

She loved that he actually did it. Crossed his heart. "Okay, I'll shut up. Personally, I'm very grateful that you're rich. I don't have to feel quite so guilty for accepting your money."

"I'm grateful, too. That I can help mitigate some of the damage."

She didn't want to tread over that territory again, so she finished off her now not-so-hot soup, and leaned back a bit to watch TV. She didn't turn up the sound, though.

AS HE WATCHED HOUSE limp around the hospital, Flynn felt pretty damn good. The conversation had gone surprisingly well. He rarely talked about his family, his father in particular. But with Willow, he'd felt at ease. Probably because she seemed to be the least judgmental person he'd ever met. Even though he'd told her what an egotistical philandering prick his father was, how he'd indiscriminately slept with nurses and patients, she hadn't batted an eye.

He wanted to know more about her in return. His gaze strayed to the jut of her breasts, covered by the sheet. But he'd already seen enough to make him hard, make him want what he was ethically bound not to take.

This was stupid and dangerous. Him being here in this room. She wasn't just a guest, she was his patient. He had a moral responsibility to treat her as such. Lying here beside her made it too easy to forget. Had he learned nothing from his father?

He abruptly straightened. "Ready for dessert?"

"Not really. I'm kind of stuffed."

"You'll change your mind by the time I get back."

"But—"

Ignoring her startled look, he quickly gathered the trays and went back to the kitchen. It only took a minute to put the dishes in the dishwasher. Then he filled the champagne bucket with ice and put four chocolate éclairs on a plate. He stared at the pastries for a second and then removed two. Couldn't he keep his head straight for a lousy five minutes? Spending any more time with her tonight would be insane. He wouldn't be rude. He'd have a glass of champagne with her, then leave her the two éclairs and excuse himself.

He quickly added a bunch of strawberries to the middle of the plate when it occurred to him that last year when he'd spent this holiday with that woman he'd met at Zabars, they'd eaten takeout Chinese and toasted beer bottles. Now he was arranging fruit.

One glass of champagne, and get the hell out.

IT HADN'T BEEN EASY, but Willow had made it into the bathroom and back to bed before Flynn showed up at the door. Freshly brushed teeth and hair made it feel a little less weird that she was entertaining from her bed. Technically his bed, but still, she was in her red see-through nightie.

He set the tray down on the dresser, then walked out, only to return a moment later carrying a champagne bucket and something she couldn't identify.

The mystery was solved as he put up yet another tray, this one a floor-standing model, next to the bed, upon which he placed their after-dinner treats.

"Strawberries and champagne," she said, all fluttery inside, and not because she liked the berries. "Very *Pretty Woman*."

"Huh?"

She laughed. "Chick-flick reference. It looks wonderful."

"I figure if we play it well, you should be both stuffed and smashed by the time the ball drops."

"A perfect ending to a relatively good year."

"It wasn't your best one, huh?" He pulled the bottle of bubbly from the bucket and faced the tray to pop the cork. Evidently, he'd done it once or twice before. As if by magic, his free hand swept up both flutes at once and he barely lost a drop before the glasses were filled.

"Wow. If you ever decide to leave medicine you'd make a hell of a sommelier."

He nodded. "Trained at my parents' dinner parties."

"They taught you to open champagne?"

He frowned, and she had this weird feeling that something was wrong. Since he'd come back with the tray, he'd barely looked at her.

"At the ripe old age of ten. Maybe nine, I'm not sure. I also learned how to make the best dry martini on the East Coast. Seriously. I think my father was as proud of that as he was my becoming a doctor."

She leaned over to take her glass from him. "Somehow I doubt that's the complete truth."

He went on to get her set up with her dessert while she thought about how much she really liked Flynn. He'd made the fruit and éclairs look nice for her, and the champagne tasted better than any champagne she'd ever had. But she couldn't get rid of the feeling that something bad was just around the corner.

8

FLYNN SETTLED BACK ON his pillow and sipped his drink. She was squared away for the evening, and he'd be out of here before midnight. He tried to figure out which episode of *House* was playing, but since his attention was mostly on the woman in the bed, it was tough going. Out of the corner of his eye, he had seen Willow pick up the chocolate éclair and lift it slowly to her mouth. He was helpless to do anything but blatantly stare as the pastry neared her lips.

From the look in her eyes, she couldn't have cared less. There was nothing in the world but Willow and her...

He jerked his gaze to the TV. He'd never really thought about the phallic shape of an éclair. But yep. It was phallic, all right. And she was really excited about it.

"Oh, God." The words were muffled, but the ecstasy was extremely clear. He'd been around women and chocolate before, so her vehemence wasn't completely unexpected. But either he was reading a lot into it, or she hadn't had an éclair in way too long.

He dared another look and found her chewing contentedly, her eyes half-closed and her lips curved in a smile. A bit of chocolate ganache rested on her plump lower lip, right at the corner of her mouth. Willow didn't realize, or didn't care.

He, being human, being male, thought about licking off that little piece of chocolate, but he wouldn't. Oh, no. He wouldn't do a thing except stop thinking about sex.

Before he could figure out a way to leave without making it seem as though he was running for his life, the tip of her tongue delicately licked up the chocolate in a neat swipe. Damn.

As a distraction, Flynn took a bite of his own pastry, and now her bliss made complete sense. As he chewed, she smiled at him before she took her next bite. He couldn't help grinning back, following her bite with his own. It was as if they were dancing a strange tango. Choreographed eating, now with extra sexual tension!

When they finished, she laughed. A great sound. "That was fun," she said. "If I didn't think it would do me in, I'd have another."

"Do you in? Are you joking? You're tougher than that."

"You go ahead. Seriously, I think one per night is my limit. Although that doesn't eliminate the possibility of having one for breakfast."

He sipped his drink, knowing she would taste of chocolate. "How about strawberries?"

"I'll try one later. Promise. Great bakery, by the way." .

"I had no idea about the goodies. I've only bought bread from them. I hope it doesn't lead to trouble."

She nodded somberly. "Pastries inevitably lead to trouble. It's part of their allure."

Even though she'd lobbed the witty banter into his court, he didn't continue the play. *Allure?* He wouldn't be able to look at an éclair again without his dick getting hard. Man, he was in a bad way. A fresh wave of lust hit him low and hard and the idea of her tasting like chocolate wasn't so much cute as erotic as hell. With one gulp, he finished his drink, then stood up. "Hey, you know, I should get going. You need your rest and I'm pretty tired myself. So, uh, I'll just put the champagne on your side and then I'll be out of your hair."

"What?" Her eyes got wide and her forehead furrowed in a look of pure disappointment. Followed quickly by confusion. "Oh, okay," she said. "That's fine."

It wasn't. He'd blundered, but only in delivery, not intent. "I can take the ice pack off, but you still need to keep your ankle elevated." Flynn had picked up the tray, but he had to stop and think where he could put it so that she could reach the champagne, but still get her crutches if she needed to go to the bathroom.

"You know what? I'll just fill your glass now." He put down the tray and turned to get the bottle, mostly to hide his utter stupidity. Just because he couldn't control himself didn't mean he had to treat her as if she had the plague. It was New Year's. They'd been having a good time. God only knew what she thought he was doing.

He couldn't keep hovering over the ice bucket. He picked up the bottle and headed around the bed. "It's nice and chilled." Inane and ridiculous, but it filled the awkward silence. "The strawberries go really well. It's actually a famous combination—"

She turned her head away.

There was no possibility he could have handled this any more poorly. His inner seventeen-year-old had taken over and turned him into a bumbling idiot. He sighed, put the champagne down on the nightstand and sat at the edge of the bed right next to Willow. "Hey."

He watched her lips press together, her hair hiding

too much of her pretty face. When she turned to him, her eyes were full of questions and, much more troubling, doubts.

"I'm sorry. I haven't handled myself very well. It's partly the situation. I mean, I don't usually cause people injury, and I've never offered my guest room to a stranger. But that's not even the real issue."

"No?" Her voice was soft, a little scared. Her hand rested on the covers. Delicate, curved and pale.

He touched her there. Not grasping, just laying his hand on hers. "I'm really attracted to you." Now that he'd decided on honesty, he wasn't at all sure how far to go. He hoped like crazy she'd give him a clue.

"You are?" Her question didn't help, but the blush that stole over her cheeks did. It made things worse.

"Yes," he said. "Very. But this is all wrong. You're my patient. It's completely unethical for me to even think of—"

She held up her other hand, stopping him. "Your patient?"

"Yes."

"Flynn, I am no such thing. Is that what's been making you act so weird? Because that's just nuts."

"You're not only here because of me, but I'm the one who's treating you."

"If all you think I am is a patient, then I'm leaving right now. Seriously."

"What else am I supposed to think?"

She closed her eyes for a moment. When she looked at him again, she shook her head. "I'll tell you what I think. I think you're a pretty decent human being. More than decent. There was an accident. You not only took responsibility, but you went way beyond the extra mile. I appreciate that, incredibly."

She hesitated then continued. "I'd also like to think that maybe you like me a little. I know, I'm being pre-sumptuous, but the truth is, I like you. And I figured, hey, if you were just feeling guilty, you'd have put me in the hospital while I recovered. Especially knowing you could afford that. At the very least you could have hired a nurse for me and gone off to Vermont. But you asked me here. You're taking care of me even though you didn't have to. That's not a doctor/patient thing, Flynn. Even you have to admit that."

WILLOW WATCHED FLYNN'S face, and she could tell he didn't quite believe her. That was confirmed with the slow shake of his head and the sadness of his smile. "I do like you. Believe that. But you're hurt. And mostly helpless. You're right, I don't want you leaving, not even with a nurse, because I am responsible for you getting better and not going broke during the process. It's going to take some time, and the potential for awk-wardness is high. If we made love and you hated it…"

"You think I might hate it?"

He stuffed his hands in his pockets, looking as if he wanted to scuff his toe in the sand. "You could."

"Does that happen a lot with you?"

"No!"

"I thought maybe there was something, you know, wrong? With your—"

"It's fine. It's great. Never better."

She grinned. Sometimes men were so easy and the poor guy was trying to be so noble it just made her ache. "I'm teasing. I get your concerns. Honestly. They're valid. They make all the sense in the world."

"Okay, then." He picked up the champagne bottle again and topped off her drink. After handing her the glass, he went to the tray and got her some strawberries on a plate. "Do you want me to go grab an éclair just in case?"

She shook her head, trying to think of a reason to ask him to ignore his sensible position. He was right. She couldn't counter even one of his arguments. The whole situation could get creepy and weird in a heartbeat. But something told her it wouldn't.

Unfortunately, she doubted he'd be persuaded by her gut feeling. Not with him being so logical and smart, and besides, the whole guilt issue was probably behind his rationale, which was something she couldn't dismiss. Just because *she* wouldn't hate it after, didn't mean *he* wouldn't.

He came back to her and put the plate on the side table. "You're all set, then?"

"Sure. I'm fine."

"Good. Okay. Well, if you need me—uh, you have a cell phone, right? I can leave that here and you could call—"

"Flynn?"

"Yeah?"

She reached over and grasped his hand. "Don't go."

He inhaled again. His fingers squeezed hers, gently, tentatively. "I'd like to stay…"

"It's just, I was having a really good time. We don't have to…you know. I can turn up the sound. We can watch whatever you like. There's all that champagne and you were telling me about the strawberries, and I'm not even a little bit sleepy. It's still so early."

"Willow…" The tone of that one word carried his no.

"Please? I won't attack you or anything. I'm incapable for one thing, but I wouldn't. How about just until I get sleepy?"

His expression changed and she knew she'd hit his

guilt button, which wasn't what she'd intended. She wasn't sure why she wanted him to stay. Why she'd begged. God, he must think she was incredibly needy. "You know what?" She withdrew her hand. "It's okay. I'm being a baby, and it's fine."

"You're not. There's no reason not to watch some TV together. And you're right. You're never gonna finish off that champagne by yourself."

She exhaled, her relief instant, although puzzling. She wanted him here. She wanted to ring in the New Year with him on her bed, if not in it.

He took the ice bucket back and filled his glass to the rim. Then the bed dipped with his weight and Willow relaxed. While it thrilled her that he was attracted to her, it was much more important that he *liked* her. Now, if she could get them back to the talking part, everything would be perfect.

9.

IT WASN'T WORKING. The level of wanting Willow was inversely proportionate to the forcefulness of the reasons why he shouldn't want her at all. The third glass of champagne had not helped. Neither did the sound from the television, his determination or his visualization of all the muscles, tendons and ligaments in the leg.

"Mmm."

Flynn rolled his eyes. It wasn't bad enough he was torturing himself, she had to sound like that? Over a strawberry?

"You're right. The combination is wonderful."

"It's something to do with the citric acid and the sweetness. Or so I've been told."

She took another sip of her drink, then another bite. Again, she moaned. He had to bite back a moan of his own. "Only an hour to go till midnight. I can take that ice pack off your ankle. Find a lower pillow. You really should get a good night's sleep, so let's make you comfortable."

Once off the bed, he felt a little better. Throwing back the covers to get to her ankle was infinitely worse. Touching her, just the barest brush with the back of his hand, threatened the last of his control.

He removed the ice pack. Slipped his hand under her ankle while he took away the pillow. Holding her gently, he lowered her foot, rubbing the pad of his thumb across her warm skin.

A surge of desire went right to his cock and he let her go, not even able to say a word as he took the ice pack straight to the kitchen. After shoving the damn thing into the freezer, he thought about climbing in after it. What the hell was going on here? This was worse than after Lisa Donald slipped him a hotel room key at the senior prom. He needed to get a grip and if that meant leaving Willow before midnight, so be it.

On his way back to the guest room, he snagged a small pillow from the couch which should make it easier for her to sleep. Then he steeled himself to do what he must. With determination and will, he put her ankle in position, tucked the covers back in place, then went to his side of the bed. He sat, drank half a glass of champagne and settled himself in to watch the New Year's Eve special from Times Square. All without looking directly at Willow.

He stretched his neck, then worked at relaxing his breathing in an effort to stop thinking about her.

Something brushed his wrist. Pure reflex made him look. Willow's hand rested on the comforter almost but not quite touching him. When he looked up, she met his gaze with dilated eyes, parted lips and want.

For a long moment, he didn't move at all. So beautiful. So near.

He reached out with one finger and stroked the side of her pinkie. It set him on fire.

WILLOW TREMBLED as he moved closer. His hand moved from the bed to brush the side of her face as he leaned in to kiss her. He tasted like champagne, and if she had her way, all kisses would be exactly like his. Warm pressure, seeking tongue, just enough push and pull and she could hardly believe it was real.

It was hard not to roll over, to touch more of his body as his fingers went to the back of her neck. But then he moved even closer until he held her tight and she was pressed against his chest. It was the safest she'd felt in a long, long time.

When he pulled back just enough to kiss the edge of her lips, her cheek, her nose, she sighed with a contentment that stilled her mind and her doubts. Whatever the consequences, she'd deal.

The way her body reacted to his touch was something new and electrifying. She moaned when his mouth went to her neck, as he licked her right there, and kissed her again. His elegant hand swept down her shoulder to her waist. He touched her breast with his fingertips.

"This is crazy," he whispered. "I've been so careful for so long."

"You're not like him," she said. "I wouldn't want you if you were."

"You don't know that."

She kissed his lips softly. "I have very good instincts."

He stared at her, his brow furrowed and his hand still. "Maybe you're right. Maybe I've been so busy trying to not be like my father that I forgot to be me."

"And maybe I'm the universe's way of helping you remember."

He kissed her, a long lovely kiss that would have made her toes curl if they could've.

"I want you," he whispered. "I want your nightgown off. I want to feel you."

She smiled, her lips so close to his. "Good. I want to

feel you, too, but you'll have to do all the work yourself."

He nodded, then pulled his shirt off. His jeans were trickier and he had to stand up, but that turned out to be nice. She liked that she could see him, see what she did to him.

His amazing body did all kinds of wonderful things to her insides, which made her hate more than ever that she had to be so careful. Just seeing his bare chest, all rugged and ripped, made her squeeze the muscles she exercised in private. She'd been so used to seeing waxed bodies in her dance classes that he seemed exotic, even though his chest hair wasn't out of control at all. Her gaze went lower, and it was her turn to swallow.

After all the debates and reasons, he slipped under the covers as if it was the most natural thing in the world. She lifted her arms so he could take off her nightie, watching his eyes darken as he looked at her.

"We can't go nuts here," he said, his voice lower and rougher. "Try to stay relaxed."

She kissed him and he pressed his body against hers. The feel of him had her pulling him closer, wanting more, wanting everything.

His hands explored, lingering on her breasts, sliding down her side and her thigh, coming back to her bottom, where he slipped inside her panties and squeezed just hard enough.

He pulled back, chasing his hands down her body, kissing and licking where he'd touched. Soon he was under the covers, teasing her gently as he went lower.

He kissed her hip, then got busy removing her panties. He could have just taken them off. Instead he made them part of the dance.

A lick here, a nibble there, a finger underneath. Each one closer to naughty, each one ratcheting up the tension in her belly as the TV continued to flicker.

Her body needed to move. She wasn't used to being so passive and it wasn't enough to touch what she could of him. He was so low on the bed she couldn't reach much. "Do you think my ankle would survive if we ditched the pillow and I scooted down?"

His head bobbed up. "No," he said in a firm yet muffled voice.

"Such a mean doctor."

He growled, at least she thought it was a growl. Whatever it was it made her smile. So did watching him move under the covers.

When he finally pulled her panties down her thighs, her eyes closed as she held her breath. He hurried at first, but new kisses slowed his path. One to the top of her thigh. One a little closer to center. Then it was just his hands and his gentleness moving her legs and carefully removing all that was left of her clothes.

He surprised her with a kiss to her foot, one that lingered a bit, and she knew it was another apology. She wished he would come up again so she could show him how deeply she didn't mind. How glad she was to be here, with him. How sometimes what looked like the worst thing could turn out amazingly well.

But she decided to relax and enjoy it as he meandered up her body. Touching, licking, nipping. Treating her knee and the outside of her thigh as if they were just as sexy as an openmouthed kiss. Which made her wonder what would happen when he moved higher.

"What are you doing to me?" she asked, not even knowing if he could hear her. She squirmed, her body lit from the inside as his hands skimmed her inner thighs. He spread her legs, careful not to jostle her ankle.

She wanted to touch him. To stroke something, anything. Since she couldn't reach him, she ended up settling for her own nipples, which were incredibly sensitive.

He took his own sweet time teasing her to death. Clearly he wanted to drive her right out of her mind with his mouth. She decided she could live with that the moment his lips landed right above her clit.

Hot breath on her wet flesh made her eyes roll and her mouth open. When his hardened tongue started exploring, she couldn't resist. She threw the covers back, needing to see him. She'd been turned on, now she quivered with desire. Every cell of her body had gotten into the act. The most difficult part was keeping her ankles relaxed. At this point, she didn't care. She'd heal.

When his fingers joined his mouth, she cried out and squeezed her nipples harder. While his tongue flicked her clit, he thrust into her. Inarticulate and needy, she squirmed and mewled, wanting some magic that would let him stay just like that and still somehow kiss her and touch her everywhere else. "More," she whispered and "Yes."

The sneak replaced his tongue with fingers from his other hand and he started traveling again. Up her belly, stopping for a swirl or a nip, then up to her ribs, all the while rubbing her clit, thrusting into her. He stopped for a second, dead still. Probably just noticing that she was tweaking her nips, squeezing them between her fingernails.

His hair tickled the underside of her breast and his tongue pushed her fingers away. As he sucked and flicked, his hand went back to driving her crazy as he rubbed her clit, fast.

Finally, she could not only see him, but touch him.

She grasped his shoulders, pulling him up, but he only moved faster, harder.

His eyes opened and held her gaze. With hair as wild as her heartbeat, he looked like sex itself. His tongue flicked rapidly at the very tip of her nipple, right in time with his finger as he brought her closer and closer to coming.

She touched him everywhere she could as she started gasping for breath, as her body went to the near edge of orgasm. Then it started. She fell past the point of no return and he didn't stop, he just kept on doing his magic. Then he kissed her. She moaned into his mouth, cried out when she felt his cock against her leg, and she came so hard there were fireworks.

MIDNIGHT WAS LONG GONE, and sleep very close. As tired as she was, Willow fought to stay awake, to keep feeling the peace of Flynn's arms around her. Her head rested on his chest and she could feel each even breath. He petted her hair, gentle rhythmic tenderness.

"You should sleep," he whispered. "Let go."

She turned a bit and kissed him. "You're as tired as I am."

He sighed. "I don't want to stop."

She kissed his chest again. Smiled into his skin. "I'm going to be here when you wake up."

"I know." His voice was deep, soft, slightly slurring with fatigue. "I'm sorry, but I'm glad. I'm glad that you're going to be here and that I get to take care of you. That makes me a bastard, but I can't help it."

"It doesn't. I'm glad, too."

His hand stilled. "This is pretty nuts. This kind of thing doesn't happen to me."

She nodded. "Me, neither."

He touched her chin, and she looked up. It was dark, but she could still see his eyes. "I like you," he said, his voice steady with intent.

"Oh."

"I wanted you to know that."

She pulled his hand to her lips and kissed his palm as a shiver ran all the way down her body. "I like you, too."

"So I was thinking," he said. "My sister's birthday is on the nineteenth. She's having a party, something with a theme that I'm going to ignore. Maybe you'd like to come with me? If you're not already booked."

She was booked in the Casa del Bradshaw, but then, he knew that. That he'd asked her was…wow. "Sure. I can do that."

"Then we're good."

"Very."

"Okay, then."

She relaxed more deeply into the warmth of his arms, and let her fingers play gently over his skin. "It's a brand-new year."

"How about that?" he whispered as he matched the rhythm of her petting.

She liked his sleepy voice. What an intimate thing to know about a person. "Started off with a bang. Pun completely intended."

His chest vibrated a bit to go with his laugh. "I have some ideas about your physical therapy."

"Oh?"

"You'll need to keep in shape while your ankle heals. Pay attention to your core muscles. I can help with that. I figure we can do some water work together. I have a big tub upstairs. Full of jets and room for two."

"You going to carry me up the stairs?"

"It's only one floor."

She squeezed his arm. "So strong. And handsome. My hero."

His fingers trailed from her hair to her cheek, where he stilled. "Why do I have the feeling you're the one who's saving me?"

Willow's breath caught for a moment. Then she kissed his chest once more before sleep came to steal her away. She didn't know what would happen, but she did know she wouldn't have to face the future alone. That he'd be there to help her. That he'd be there.

She really was the luckiest person ever.

* * * * *

Ms. Sing

1

"TAXI!"

Maggie Trent waved down the Yellow Cab as she avoided the slush at the curb. At least it wasn't snowing at the moment. She climbed in the backseat, put her big bag next to her and gave the address to the driver.

Just saying the street made her shiver with anticipation and excitement. She was on her way to the audition of her life. One that, if she got the part, would change everything. She squeezed her hands together before she took off her gloves. It was cold in the cab, but she'd need her fingers to get her fare from her purse.

She shouldn't be this excited, not if she didn't want to jinx things. The chances in general of getting a callback, let alone a part, were incredibly slim. Especially in a musical with this pedigree. Every singer, actor and dancer in New York would be dying for a role. But she had an ace in the hole. At least she hoped so. She knew the librettist. Well. And she'd worked with him on the play. Her practical experience might have been limited to off-off Broadway and college productions, but Randy liked her for the part. No guarantees, he'd said, and she knew he wasn't joking, but still. He liked her for the part.

With her job, it hadn't been easy to get to auditions but that would all change after today, for better or for worse. If she got the nod for a callback, she would pass up the promotion that would send her to Washington, D.C., and really, truly give her singing career a shot. If she didn't make the cut…

She wouldn't think like that. Miracles happened. It was New Year's Eve Day, and she had a week's vacation in front of her so that was auspicious, right? New beginnings? Fresh resolve?

She'd selected a Sondheim number for her first piece. Everyone knew he was the most difficult to sing, and she wanted to start with a bang. If they let her sing another, she was ready there, too, with a piece from *Chess*.

Her stomach tightened at the thought. Yep, she'd been right to skip breakfast.

As the cab slowed to a crawl in the late morning traffic, Maggie's cell rang. It was underneath her shoes and her makeup bag, of course, and it better not be work with an emergency. Hmm. Colin. He shouldn't be calling her now. With a sigh she flipped open the phone. "What's wrong?"

"The idiot's done it again. I swear, Maggie, I'm going to wring his bloody neck."

All the air went out of her lungs as she imagined the worst. Colin's twin brother, Blake, was in Afghanistan where he was covering the Middle East for the BBC. "What's happened?"

"He's gone missing. He checked in four days ago from north of Kabul. He'd made a connection with a contact in the insurgency. He was supposed to call in two days ago, and he hasn't."

"Oh, God. How's your mother?"

"Scared. As usual. He does this every—" Colin stopped and she could practically see him eye the wall, ready to throw his fist into it. "His boss has no idea where the hell he is. No one does."

The cab turned the corner, and there was the building where the audition was being held. People were standing in line outside, all of them bundled up from the cold, but she knew they were sweating with nerves and excitement. That was the thrilling part about these big calls. Anything was possible.

She held back a sigh. This was her do-or-die audition and she was only two blocks away. Perhaps she could go in for just a moment, maybe to sing one song—her chest tightened and she hated that she'd hesitated for even a second. There simply wasn't another choice. It was Colin. "I'm on my way."

"When I find him," he said, "I'm going to kill him myself." Then he hung up.

The cab moved forward and instead of telling the driver to take the next right, her breath caught in her throat. She was so close. It wasn't that she hated her life now, she didn't. Working for Homeland Security's New York office was important and meaningful, but it wasn't her dream. Not her biggest dream, at least. She'd been singing all her life, fantasizing about her Broadway debut. She'd practiced her Tony acceptance speech every year, even though she'd never been eligible. This could have changed it all. It could have kept her in New York. Kept her close to Colin. It could have been her miracle.

She tapped on the partition. "Change of plans," she said, then gave him Colin's address. She sat back and closed her eyes, not able to watch as the cab turned away.

Damn Blake. Did the man have no sense of self-preservation? No thought for anyone but himself? The insurgency had no qualms about killing a British journalist. They'd proved it several times. And of course, Colin had to be the one to pick up the pieces.

She stared blankly out the window as they drove straight past where she lived, heading to Colin's apartment in a very nice section of the Meatpacking District.

Her own place was tiny, dark and, frankly, a nightmare. Colin had been horrified when he'd first seen it. He'd gone so far as to offer her the guest room at his place, which was possibly the worst suggestion ever. Which he knew, but the man hated the idea of worrying about her. He had enough on his plate.

As she passed Ninth Avenue, her thoughts drifted to simpler times. Back to Cambridge University, where she'd met Colin and his twin. They'd lived a block away from her student lodging, roughing it. Their father was a diplomat, a real mover and shaker on the international scene and Colin was meant to follow in his footsteps. The brothers had shared a place at university while Blake studied English and Colin international relations and languages. It had been friendship at first sight. As the three amigos, they'd fallen in and out of love with various and sundry, studied, laughed and annoyed each other endlessly. Through it all and three years later, they were still the best of friends.

Maggie shifted as the cab made another turn. She tried to remember what it was like to be that carefree, to be that hopeful about everything. Back then, when she pictured her future, it was all about Broadway success and true love with Colin. That boy had stolen her heart from the beginning. Sadly, she'd never gotten it back.

He'd changed so much from those days. He'd been incredibly adventurous, taking her to clubs and on impromptu trips to France or Spain. He'd been devoted to modern art and jazz guitar, and they'd spent so many nights talking about philosophy and politics. She'd changed, too. Her world had narrowed to singing and work. Singing, work and Colin. Work was the only one that had shown real signs of success.

Blake, on the other hand, hadn't changed at all. There was a lot to be said for his exuberance, but his behavior had long ago gone from forgivably daring to outright recklessness.

Even so, she missed him. He'd nursed her through the long days and nights of abject misery when Colin had gotten engaged to Elizabeth, and for that Maggie would always be grateful.

Even from war zones, Blake called her regularly, if infrequently, checking to make sure she wasn't still pining over his brother. Of course, she hadn't told him the truth, but then he didn't need to be told.

The cab pulled up in front of Colin's building. She gave the driver his money and hurried past the doorman into the lobby. She passed by the sign-in; they knew her here. Perhaps well enough to read the anxiety in her expression because Will didn't say hello and neither did Sonny.

The ride up to the fourth floor felt longer than the drive, but finally, she was at Colin's door. He flung it open, a phone at his ear, his face composed, his body tense as a bow string.

After plopping her bag and coat down, she traded her huge boots for more practical but less comfortable heels, then went straight to the kitchen and put on the kettle as she listened in on his conversation.

"...Colin Griffith," he said, using his most formidable voice. "The man I'm looking for is Fahran Azimi. He's a student, but he often works with members of the Associated Press." He stopped speaking. "I know precisely what the hour is there." The pacing stopped. "Yes, it is inconvenient to hunt this man down. War is inconvenient. Your people are the best equipped to do the hunting." His lips were pressed together tightly, which for Colin was the calm before the storm. "All you need to understand, Mr. Foster, it that Mr. Azimi needs to be located immediately and quietly." He paused and his body relaxed a bit. "Yes, that's correct. You have my number."

Maggie leaned against the kitchen door, watching him. He closed his phone, but didn't turn to her. Knowing him, he was mentally going through his list of who he'd call next, what strings could be pulled. And even though she was heartsick at missing the audition, she was glad she'd come. He would move mountains if she needed him for anything, but lately he hadn't seemed to need her quite as often.

It was the expectations. From his parents, from all those important people who'd been part of his meteoric rise in public service. Since his brother delighted in thumbing his nose at everyone who cared about him and destroying his family's reputation, Colin had become the default standard-bearer.

"I can't think of anything more I can do." He still hadn't turned to her.

"I'm making tea." Around him, she tended to speak with a soupçon of a British accent, even though she'd been born in Virginia. But as she'd learned from traveling around the world with her family, she tended to mimic all accents.

Finally, he came over to her and gave her a one-armed hug. She rubbed his back a bit until the kettle whistled. Ever since Cambridge, fixing tea had become almost a sacred thing. Whenever there were discussions or problems, the kettle went on.

She doubted Colin had eaten, so while the leaves steeped in his old pot, she put together a tray of snacks. Some cookies, cheese and crackers, toast and jam. Unlike herself, Colin didn't eat under stress. She'd force him to, though. He looked like hell.

The cups and food went on the tray and she brought it all out to the coffee table in the living room, where she found him staring at her. "What?"

"Nothing. Just, you look great."

She inhaled; said nothing. Just smiled as she sat down. But his compliment had jolted her with the reminder of the audition. It was happening right now. Without her. Tears burned at her eyes, which she quickly swiped away. It wasn't as if she had a real chance at getting the part. Even if Randy had thought she was the best thing since sliced bread, there were still the director, the producers. But dammit. She'd tried harder at singing than any other thing in her life, with the possible exception of learning Mandarin Chinese. Of course she knew she was good at languages. She only hoped she was good enough for Broadway. Now, she'd never know.

Maybe it was for the best. Maybe not knowing if she was good enough was a blessing. Besides, there were worse things than the demise of a ridiculous dream. Such as your twin brother being held by enemy insurgents in Afghanistan.

When she glanced up, Colin's stare was no longer focused on her red dress. It was a stare she'd come to know well over the past couple of years. There was no disrespect or dismissal in that look. Just that his thoughts were elsewhere. She understood. Even though she never looked at him without seeing too much. Wanting— Dammit. She wouldn't think about that now.

Talk about foolish dreams. "Come on," she said. "Drink some tea. Talk to me."

He cleared his throat as if that would also clear his thoughts, then joined her on the couch.

She poured, his with two lumps and milk, then put some cheese and crackers on his saucer along with his cup. "Eat, please. You need to be at your best."

He nodded although he didn't obey. He just closed his eyes. "This is all so typical. I should just let it go. Let the chips fall where they may. Everyone always cleans up after Blake and it's high time we all stopped. That I stopped. If he's gotten himself into trouble, he'll have to suffer the consequences."

"You know, it might not be all that dire. He could be out of touch because of his location or because of an equipment malfunction."

"That would be convenient, but really, it doesn't even matter anymore. Blake didn't tell his boss where he was going. He knew what danger he was heading for, and he did it anyway."

"You're right. He's an idiot. But he has a way of always landing on his feet. He'll get out of this. And who knows, maybe this will be his wake-up call."

Colin frowned as he sipped his tea. "Stupid stubborn bastard."

"Yes, he is."

For the first time that morning, Colin smiled. "Thank you. I don't know what I'd do if you weren't here."

"I wouldn't be anywhere else."

"I know."

She picked up a piece of toast, hoping he'd do the same. But her stomach rebelled at the thought of food, and in spite of herself, she discretely glanced at her watch as she returned the toast to her plate. Her gaze went back to Colin, unshaven, his hair an utter mess, and she thought again how much he'd changed since they'd first met.

He'd run into her. Literally. He was playing American football of all things, a game of touch, when he'd gone long and smashed into her as he'd caught the ball. She'd been flattened but unhurt, and he'd fussed over her so much she'd almost decked him. They'd ended up laughing and while his friends called for the ball, he'd asked her all kinds of questions, mostly about where she was from and what she was studying and why she'd come to England to attend university. They'd spoken French at each other, then Mandarin, followed by Italian. He'd thought he'd got her with Egyptian, but she'd lived there for two years, so it was four-four. Then he'd spouted two more languages and she only had one. It was close enough to warrant an exchange of numbers.

She'd been excited because he was the best-looking guy she'd met in England, and all that talking made her think he'd been flirting. He towered over her and was altogether too wiry for her taste, but there was something incredibly sexy about him. The way he ran his hand through his dark hair, his amazing cheekbones. He'd made her giggle. She'd been mortified, but helpless to stop.

She wasn't the only grad student in love with Colin. It seemed as if every girl at Cambridge had made a fool of herself over him or his twin, and if it hadn't been for Blake, Maggie would have done the same. Because Colin had Elizabeth. She was a proper British beauty—complete with title—and appropriate for Colin in every way.

So Maggie had become friends with the twin brothers, and when Colin had told her he'd gotten a job in New York, she'd been ecstatic.

Colin put his cup back on the table and blinked at her. "Didn't you have something on today?"

She kept her expression neutral. "No. Nothing," she said. "It's New Year's Eve Day. That's probably what you're thinking."

"No, it was something—oh, shit. Your audition." He looked at his watch. "You can still make it, can't you?"

"I'm not leaving." She glanced at her own watch again in some stupid hope that she'd misread the time. She hadn't. "Doesn't matter. I never stood a chance."

"You don't know that. I'm sure they'll make an exception. I'll call—"

"Your diplomatic friends have no sway over Broadway musicals, but thank you," she said wryly. "Can we drop it?" He looked stricken, and she was afraid she might start crying again. "When did you find out about Blake?"

He frowned at the abrupt change of subject, looked as if he wanted to argue further, but then fought against a yawn. "Uh, four this morning."

"I know you haven't eaten, but did you at least shower?"

"Why? Do I smell?"

"No. I just think it would do you some good."

He shook his head.

"I'll be here. I'll bring the phone to you if something happens. You know I will."

He glanced down at his wool pants and white shirt. No tie, but he'd dressed as if he might need to run to the consulate at a moment's notice. "I didn't get to sleep until two. Bad luck."

"You? On a school night?"

That made him laugh, but he still didn't move.

"Go. Shower. Wash that horrible hair."

He grunted as he got up and when he passed her, he squeezed her shoulder.

She smiled until he was out of the room.

2

IT FELT WONDERFUL to stand under the hot water. The morning had been a nightmare, but he needed to relax. Thank goodness for Maggie. He hated that she'd missed such a great chance, but he was glad she was here. Always practical, more calming than any shower, she was his rock. She knew more about his situation than anyone outside of London, outside of family. But then, Maggie was family. He certainly preferred her over his irresponsible brother.

Colin's head dropped to his chest as a wave of exhaustion hit. Maybe Blake had the right idea after all. Live hard, party hard and leave a handsome corpse. When was the last time *he'd* done anything crazy? Or spontaneous? Blake always managed to get what he was after, didn't he? The bastard was so charming everyone always forgave him and, in the end, that's what mattered. Except that wasn't quite true, was it?

The shampoo bottle was in Colin's hand so he put some in his hair and washed as he tried not to think about Blake. Instead, he thought again about how she'd looked in that red dress. She should wear it more often. Show herself off. She needed to get out there, have herself a life. Find someone.

Not just anyone. My God, who could possibly be good enough for Maggie? No one he knew. Blake had tried to tell him that he should have a go, but Colin had laughed. Maggie and he were friends, and he wasn't about to go blundering about with that at stake.

No, he was damned lucky to have her in his corner. How many nights had she comforted him after that messy breakup with Elizabeth? Her faith in his abilities had been pivotal in his career thus far. No, he wasn't about to put any of that at risk. And that, right there, was the difference between himself and his brother.

Anxious to get back out to the phone, even though he knew Maggie was as good as her word, he washed quickly. He ended up putting on a different suit, something he could comfortably wear on a transatlantic flight. Just in case.

The sight of her in the kitchen was like a balm. She'd taken charge, replenishing the tea, and setting his cell phone by his seat. "Did anyone call?"

"No. It's been quiet. I turned on BBCA, but nothing. I assume you spoke to his boss?"

"Yes, twice." Colin sat at the table and picked up half an egg salad sandwich. "He's got every journalist in the country looking for him. Blake's so cagey, no one knows where to look. The fool didn't have an armed escort, which is suicidal."

"Everything will be okay." Maggie sat beside him and put her hand on his. "You wait. He'll have some crazy story about how he'd gotten the story of a lifetime, and snuck out with no one the wiser. Knowing him, he'll probably win a Pulitzer Prize for it."

Colin stared at her hand. It was lovely and comforting and the feel of her made sense when nothing else did. "He's not eligible."

"I imagine they'd make an exception for him. Everyone does."

"They do, don't they?"

"He tried to fool me the first time I met him, did you know?"

Her hand hadn't moved, but somehow she'd gotten closer so he could see her eyes clearly. They were blue-green and almond-shaped, one of her best features. She wasn't a flashy beauty like Elizabeth, but she was very pretty. In fact, she could be downright striking when she put her mind to it. Most often, she didn't get all made up, but today she had. For the audition. He registered what she'd just told him. "Fooled you how?"

She slipped her hand from his and poured them both some Earl Grey. "I'd called you a couple of days after we met. I figured we could go to the language center together. I didn't know it then, but Blake answered, pretended to be you and had me come over."

"The shit."

She grinned. "I knew right away he wasn't you."

"How? He could even fool our parents when he wanted to."

"He spoke rotten Italian."

"You never told me about that."

"I thought I had."

A sudden sickening thought occurred to him. "He didn't… You two didn't…"

"No. What a question."

"We're talking about Blake," Colin said drily as he picked up his cup, a sudden and fierce possessiveness taking him by surprise. Maggie was as much Blake's friend as she was his, so what the hell was that about?

"Yeah, but I'm part of that equation, and frankly, I'm insulted." She lifted her chin. "When did you last speak to your parents?"

"A couple of hours ago."

"That's an hour too long."

Colin sighed. She was right, of course. Maggie normally was.

SHE WASHED THE FEW DISHES from their meal as she wondered which one of them was the bigger idiot. Her for wishing Colin would see her as more than a friend, or him for being so blind. As if she'd have slept with Blake. He was a great as a friend, but he couldn't keep it in his pants. Although, to his credit, he was up-front about his intentions, so none of his conquests seemed to mind.

As for Colin, he'd never been one to sleep around, just as she hadn't been. He'd been dating Elizabeth for only a few months before Maggie had met him. Which was fine because being his friend was great. What would she do without him? She'd wondered for a long time what would have happened if they'd met earlier, but she'd gotten her answer after he and Elizabeth had broken up. Colin saw her as a friend, and only that.

She probably should have distanced herself when he came to New York. It would have been easier then. Work kept her busy, that was a good excuse. She could have made up a boyfriend, or even better, had an actual boyfriend, but no. She had clung to the fantasy that he'd look up one day and it would strike him like lightning that they were meant for each other. God.

Could she be a bigger dolt? She still blushed when she thought of how excited she'd been after the big breakup. How she'd felt so sure. But all he'd done was get hideously drunk and tell her she was a fine bloke. He'd used the word *bloke*. It had nearly killed her.

Oh, who was she kidding? Given the choice, she'd go through it again. All the pain, all the embarrassment. Because the thought of living a life with no Colin was too painful to contemplate. So what would it be like when she moved to Washington, D.C.? They'd talk, of course, at least twice a week. Maybe see each other every other month. Until he found another girlfriend.

The thought nearly squeezed the life out of Maggie. Which was completely silly. What did she expect? He would meet someone. Especially after she was gone and he had more time on his own.

She closed her eyes. Angry with herself. Angry with Colin. Furious with Blake. He'd pop up as if nothing had happened. Her chance at the audition would be over. Her excuse for turning down the promotion in D.C. vanished.

Colin's voice filtered into the kitchen as he walked nearer. Not that she could make out the words, but she didn't have to. She knew what his talks were like with his parents. Very civil, very calm, no matter what. Because it was Colin's job to be the grown-up. His mother liked her sherry a bit too much and was constantly in a panic. His father was so busy with his politics and his horses and his expectations that poor Colin was always trying to appease one or both of them. Trying to be twice as good to make up for Blake's rebellions.

For all that, the brothers loved each other. Needed each other. Maggie hoped that in time, Colin would let himself relax and be a little more like Blake, and Blake would grow up and become more like Colin. If Blake lived long enough, it could work out perfectly.

She dried her hands and her thoughts went yet again to her own lost opportunity. The last thing she needed was to have it haunt her in her new job. Moving to D.C. would solve a lot of her problems. Money was only one thing. Leaving Colin was a much bigger deal.

It's not that she wouldn't see him. He came to Washington a lot. He even had a pied-à-terre off Dupont Circle. But she wouldn't see him as often, and that was both good and bad. The move could be—should be— the perfect time to get over him once and for all. She just wondered if she'd be strong enough to do that if he kept popping up. Anyway, that was something to think about later, after they'd found Blake.

Colin came into the kitchen but he didn't sit down. "She was glad I called. You were right. She was worried that I wasn't telling her something bad. She says thanks for taking care of me."

"I suppose you didn't mention we were taking care of each other."

"No. I wouldn't lie to my mother."

She went to him and bumped her shoulder to his. "Stupid git."

"Hey!" He bumped her back.

"Have you told Elizabeth?"

He stopped. "No. Should I?"

"That's up to you, but despite everything she's been a good friend to Blake."

He stared at the table for several seconds. "I'm not going to worry her yet. Let's wait till tonight."

"She probably won't be home. It's New Year's Eve."

"Oh. Well. I don't want to ruin her plans. It can wait, I think."

Maggie shook her head. It wouldn't occur to him that *she* might have had plans for the night, but that wasn't his fault. She was always there when Colin called. And here she had such a high IQ. Where had she gone wrong?

Colin stretched his neck with a wince. "I should call Foster back and see if he's gotten anywhere. Although I don't want to piss him off."

"Come on." She grabbed his hand and pulled him into the living room and onto the big ottoman by the couch. "Sit."

"Why?"

"You're too tense. I'm going to work on your neck."

He opened his mouth as if to argue, then closed it again, his shoulders sagging. "You're too good to me."

"I know. Take off your shirt."

"Cheeky."

"That's me. I never take no for an answer."

His shirt came off, and of course he folded it before tossing it on the couch. He wasn't as thin as he'd been in college. There were actual muscles now. Long and lean, but wiry and tough, with a great chest. And then there was that gorgeous face of his with his sharp cheekbones and strong chin.

Why did she do this to herself?

"I'll be back," she said as she hurried away.

"Where are you going?"

"To get lotion." She probably didn't have time for a cold shower. Which was a joke. That never had worked.

She knew there was nothing useable in his guest bathroom, so she went into his en suite. There was a full bottle of a very fruity-smelling lotion under the sink, but she didn't imagine he'd enjoy that, and the whole point was for him to relax. There was, however, an unopened plastic bottle of baby oil in the back. Why he would have this was a mystery, probably something she didn't want to know, but it would do the job nicely.

He had slumped forward, elbows on knees, when she got back to him. "Maybe we should do this in a prone position?"

"I think I'd be more relaxed here. I don't want to fall asleep."

"I would wake you, if anything—"

"I know." He looked up at her, his face troubled. "Thank you for this."

She shrugged. It wasn't their first massage. She'd gone to school for it and had used her skills in three countries when she'd needed extra cash, which was pretty much always. The secret was to keep the information quiet. Once someone knew she'd been a professional, especially a friend, it was hard to tell them to screw off. If she'd wanted to be a masseuse, she'd have become one.

Colin never asked. Not once. Blake, all the time.

Before she started, she handed him a towel and then rolled up her sleeves. She liked that he liked her dress. She'd found it in Milan and had spent too much on it, but the red made her feel powerful and the slinky skirt made her feel sexy, both of which she needed to audition. After kicking off her shoes, she poured some oil in her hand before warming her palms.

The moment she touched his skin, he sighed and his shoulders lowered. But she didn't get into real trouble until she went deeper.

She'd given him massages at least a dozen times over the years. Each time, he'd been completely silent and thanked her profusely after.

This time, he moaned long and low. It was the exact sound she heard when she dreamed of them making love.

3

THE FEEL OF HER WARM hands pressing into his shoulders fell right on the border between pleasure and pain, and his moan escaped before he could stop it. Maggie had told him that's where he held his tension, and she'd proved it often enough. Yet it never occurred to him to consciously loosen up. How could he? This massage would help, but to truly relax, he'd have to do something drastic—say, run off to Tahiti.

She hit a particularly sore bit, and he found himself angry again that Blake had tried to seduce Maggie when they'd met. She'd denied it, but Colin knew better. Maggie had all the qualities Blake sought. Brilliant, funny, irreverent, sly. Together, the two of them would have been unstoppable.

"Relax," she said, stopping for a moment. "Don't think. Just let go."

He took a deep breath and let it out slowly. His eyes had closed the moment she'd touched him, and he felt every bit of his weariness. There'd been so much tension at the consulate of late. On the international front, of course, but there was also a great deal of internal politics snaking its way through the ranks. He tried not to get involved, but there was no way to stay completely out of it.

Blake would have told him to quit and go where the

real action was. Damn him. He wasn't truly happy unless his life was in imminent danger. He breathed deeply once more before Maggie could say anything.

"Good boy," she whispered. "Put down your head, I'm going to work on your neck."

He did, and her fingers went up to the base of his skull. This time, he was able to bite off his moan, but only just. She had magic hands. It was a treat whenever she'd offer to give him a massage. He never asked. He'd seen her reaction when others presumed. Insensitive jerks. That list was headed by his boneheaded brother.

Thank God the two of them hadn't gotten together. The last thing Maggie needed was someone who would dash off to a war zone or jump off bridges or race motorcycles. She deserved someone who would be there for her. Maybe it wasn't as exciting, but there was a lot to be said about a steady head and long-term goals.

"Relax. You're doing it again."

He let out the breath he hadn't realized he'd been holding. Just the idea of Maggie and Blake…

"Colin. The phone's right here. There's no more you can do, at least for now. So focus, would you?"

He shook out his arms and recommitted to relaxation. He needed to get rid of this damn headache, and her fingers in his hair was better than any pill.

Once his head was back down and she was using the pads of her thumbs to mesmerize and calm, his thoughts drifted from his newest art acquisition, a Basquiat that he'd hung in the bedroom, to Maggie's red dress. Then he imagined fingers at her zipper and the way her long auburn hair would look on her bare back as the dress fell.

He stiffened immediately, furious that Blake might have touched her that way, but he caught himself short.

"What was that about? Are you all right?"

"I'm fine. Sorry."

"No problem. Concentrate on your breathing, okay? In for five, out for seven."

"I'll do my best."

Counting commenced, and for a while it worked. He didn't think about anything but his lungs, his diaphragm, the warmth of her hands, of her body so close behind him. Was that her breast brushing against his back?

Moaning again, this time out of pure desperation, he lifted his head. "This isn't working. I can't relax."

Maggie stopped, then stepped around to face him. "I had you, then I lost you. What happened?"

"I can't still my brain. It's no use."

"Okay, then let's do this. You put up with me for ten more minutes. I want to finish your shoulders. I promise not to go a second over, but I know you. If you try, you can relax for ten minutes." She went behind him again, although she didn't touch him.

He wanted to take advantage of her skills. To let her help him. Instead, he stood up, scaring a surprised yelp out of Maggie. Spinning round, he saw why. She'd been pouring oil, which was now all down the front of her dress.

"Oh, shit, Maggie, I'm sorry. I didn't mean to—"

She held out the bottle of oil. "Please take this. It's dripping on the carpet. And so am I." She lifted the hem of her dress to contain the damage as she hustled off to his bedroom.

He cursed his way into the kitchen. Could nothing go right today? Where the hell was his brother? "Shit," he said again as his head throbbed in time to his heartbeat.

MAGGIE GROANED AS SHE looked at the wreckage. The oil had spilled down the bodice and the skirt. Why did it have to be her favorite dress? Why hadn't he warned her he was going to stand up?

She unzipped and stepped out of the dress and put it on the bathroom counter. Now in her panties and bra, she felt exposed and that made her angrier.

She looked under his cupboards for talcum powder, but she hadn't seen any in her search for the oil, and nothing had changed. She rose, did her own breathing exercise until she calmed down, then opened the bathroom door. "Colin?"

"Yes?"

She jumped at the nearness of his voice. He was in his bedroom. "Could you please bring me some cornstarch? I'm sure you have some in the kitchen. If not in the right cupboard, there should be some under the sink."

"Right. Cornstarch."

She shut the door again as he dashed off. She really didn't understand him sometimes. How could a man so utterly confident at work, in crises that involved nations, get so lost in his own kitchen?

His mother, of course. And the nannies. Neither of the boys had lifted a finger taking care of themselves. Not that they didn't have to work. Every summer from the time they were teens they had to have jobs, all volunteer work, helping others. It was part of their family's code. They had great privilege and therefore they had to do everything they could to earn it by giving back to the community.

But Maggie wouldn't be surprised if it took Colin an hour to find the cornstarch. He had a maid in twice a week, his groceries were delivered and he never cooked.

His clothes were professionally cleaned. He still had nannies.

His parents had done a lot right, though. He was a selfless man. Oblivious at times, but honestly good. He still donated time and money to all kinds of causes and he mentored two U.K. college students who attended university.

Oh, who was she kidding? She couldn't be mad at him on a good day.

"I've found it."

She opened the door just enough to grab the box. "Thanks. And could you get me something to put on?"

"Oh, yes. I'm sure I have something."

The last of his sentence trailed off as he wandered toward the closet.

As for her, she spread the dress carefully on the counter, then evenly sprinkled the powder all over the stain. It took quite a lot of the box, and she might have to do it again if it didn't blot up everything. It would be hours, if not overnight, before she would know if the remedy had worked.

He knocked again. "This should do it."

She held her hand out from behind the door and pulled back his big burgundy robe. It was thick and would certainly keep her warm. It also dragged on the floor, not to mention fell way past her hands. She looked like Dopey from *Snow White.* "Colin?"

"Is it all right?"

"It's really long. Maybe you have something shorter?"

"Ah. I'll look."

She took off the robe. It would serve him right if she marched out of here in her underwear. He'd have a stroke, even if they were her best set. Black and lacy, they were another crucial part of her confidence-for-auditions armory.

The reminder made her ache, but she stopped herself. That ship had sailed. Which meant that after this was over, she'd have to tell Colin that she was moving. Her legs wobbled at the thought.

"Try this," he said.

They traded clothing, and this time she brought back one of his white Oxford shirts. She hesitated, but the fabric felt wonderful. Donning the thing, she realized it actually did work, coming down to about mid-thigh. The sleeves had to be rolled up, but that wasn't a big deal. It actually covered a lot more than her bathing suit or some of her summer dresses, and he'd seen her in those.

The only real problem was that it made her think of all those movie images where the girl seduces the boy wearing his big white shirt.

Terrific. The day couldn't get any better.

After a heartfelt sigh, she left the bathroom and almost ran right into Colin.

He stepped back quickly. "Is it salvageable?"

"I think so. It's going to take a while to know for sure," she said, concentrating on getting the sleeves rolled up to a comfortable length.

"I'm sorry."

"Don't worry about it. It's just a dress." Just an audition. Just her life.

"You looked beautiful in it."

That stopped her. That was twice now. He complimented her all the time, but not about her looks. After all, she was still that good bloke he could turn to in bad times. "Thanks."

She slowly looked up to see he was staring at her

legs. His gaze moved all the way down to her bare feet, then slowly back up her body. It took him a long time to reach her face. When their eyes met, his face flushed.

"Don't blame me," she said, as self-conscious as she'd ever been and also unnervingly pleased. "You got me into this mess."

His mouth opened, but no words followed.

"I'm getting myself a drink." She turned, let herself grin like a fool as she walked—no, sashayed—out of the bedroom.

4

THINGS WEREN'T MAKING SENSE. Or rather, he wasn't making sense. Colin went back to the living room where his half-dressed friend was fixing cocktails.

He had no business thinking about her legs. It simply wasn't smart. He'd made every effort to keep his and Maggie's relationship free of the mess of sex. He'd seen vivid proof that friends with benefits didn't last. All one had to do was look at his brother's life. The man went through women as if they were library books, and while Blake said he preferred it that way, he wasn't the picture of happiness and stability, was he?

Colin was nothing if not practical. He wanted Maggie around for the long run. There was no way to predict if they'd be sexually compatible or good at being a couple. He knew she was an amazingly fine friend. End of discussion. Wanting her was counterproductive. And yet…

"Here you go."

He turned to find she'd snuck up behind him, her bare feet quiet on the carpet. He tended to forget how much shorter she was than him. The top of her head barely reached his eyes.

He took the scotch from her hand and had a good sip. She'd known what to pour for him just as he knew she'd fixed herself a bourbon and Seven. He kept a stock of

7-Up in the wet bar cooler for her. He also made sure he always had those awful sandwich cookies she liked so much, because she'd never buy them for herself, but she always ate them here. On the holidays he stocked good chocolates, only the nuts and chews, never creams, for the same reason. He wanted Maggie happy.

He wished he could do something about her musical ambitions, but there he was at a loss. Elizabeth had told him not to worry, that getting a singing job in the theater was very rare, but he would have liked to give her a hand up.

"What's going on?" Maggie turned her head to look at him, her gaze worried.

"It's hard to think clearly, that's all. I'd try to sleep if I knew it wouldn't be useless."

"I know. All I can tell you is to have faith. He's a smart cookie. He'll come home."

"I did some research on twins, you know." He sat down on the couch, putting his cell on the cushion beside him. "We aren't typical."

She sat across from him in the wing chair and crossed her legs. The shirt went even higher on her thigh. She pulled it down a bit, but it didn't help. "I could have told you that, but what makes you odd twins?"

He made sure to look at her face. "Even though we're identical, our temperaments are more opposite than alike. Even as infants, according to rumor, we were night and day."

"I imagine he was a handful."

Colin nodded. "And I was a perfect angel. Again, rumor. I have no recollection."

She laughed. "All that matters is that you're not a perfect angel now. That would be insufferable."

"I'm glad my flaws please you."

"They do. But go on. What else?"

"The moment we were dressing ourselves we wanted to be as unique as possible, unlike most twins. We never had anything like a secret language, or even shorthand. Blake was always running around snooping or getting into trouble, and I wanted to be a footballer and applied myself to the task."

"So you're the yin to his yang, or vice versa. I used to know what those really meant, but my mind has been slipping for years."

"It has not. You do that a lot, you know. Excuse yourself for things that aren't the least bit true."

"I do not."

"Who would know better than me?"

She paused to sip on her drink. "No one."

"There, you see?"

"I think I'm going to take back that not insufferable thing."

"Too late."

She smiled. "I don't know any other twins. You two seem just right to me."

"According to the experts we're rubbish. Even twins raised continents apart are better at it than we are."

She shrugged, making the shirt dip down over her left shoulder, revealing her black bra strap. "What do experts know?"

He swallowed too much and coughed for a while, his nose and throat burning. That would teach him.

"You all right?"

He wanted to tell her that no, he wasn't in the least bit all right. She had no business taking off her dress when he was so distracted and why couldn't she just put up with the length of the much more appropriate robe? He nodded.

"I'm not," she said. "I'm antsy and I don't know what to do with myself."

"I understand."

"Between us, we should be able to think of something."

He had thought of something: forgetting all the reasons he and Maggie should only be friends. She looked even better in his shirt than she had in the red dress. Her hair seemed a darker red, her skin fairly glowed. He'd always thought she was attractive, but lately it had been on his mind a lot. It would have been so much easier if she had a man in her life. Or maybe it would have been unbearable.

He stood, needing some distance. A distraction. There weren't enough rooms in his flat. He would call Blake's boss. Find out if he'd heard anything at all.

Maggie picked up the remote control for the TV over the fireplace. It was already on BBCA but it wasn't the news, it was a repeat of a *Doctor Who* episode with David Tennant. Nice chap. Scot. They'd met at a charity dinner.

"Isn't there an all-day BBC news channel?" she asked.

"Yes," he said. "But not on my feed."

"Figures." She left the remote and headed for the bar.

He dialed Blake's boss, but it went to voice mail and he hung up in disgust. Maggie returned, brushing her sleeve against his and the urge to touch her flared inside him. "Do you think your dress is better now?"

Her mouth opened briefly and she turned away. "I doubt it, but I'll go see."

"Wait," he said, catching her arm. "What is it?"

"Nothing."

He turned her to face him square on, and he could see he'd been correct.

She let out a breath. "If you want me to leave, just say the word."

"Of course I don't want you to leave."

Her blush made her lovely. Lovelier. "The dress? It's only been about fifteen minutes."

"Oh. Well. Then don't bother with it. I just thought you might be more comfortable."

"You're lying."

"I'm not."

"Who would know better than me?"

No one. Ever. "It's the scotch, that's all."

Maggie looked down at his hand, still holding her arm. It was a tight hold, one that would hurt in a minute if he wasn't careful. The scotch story was complete bull, that she knew. He could handle his liquor, just as he could handle almost any situation. His family drove him crazy, but then that was true for everyone. "Colin?"

He dropped his hand. "Shit."

"It's all right. You have a free pass today. Okay? At least until Blake checks in."

His brow lifted, transforming his expression into one she hadn't seen before. "You mean I can get away with anything?"

She eyed him for a minute, not sure what to make of the lower pitch of his voice, the way his gaze had darkened. Her skin tingled with awareness. The sudden tension had to be her imagination…

He leaned forward and oh, God, he was going to— No. He thrust out his nearly empty glass. "Yes, I'll have another. Thank you."

There was no denying she felt disappointed, but she didn't let it show. Chiding herself for being foolish, she simply took his glass.

He went back to pacing as she got to the wet bar. It

was a beautiful thing, that bar, and it was sorely under-used. He rarely drank, she never did when she had to work the next day. She loved that there was always 7-Up and how he kept the much despised Baileys on hand because she enjoyed one from time to time.

It was so like him.

And so unlike Blake. That bastard never had anything on hand. Never had any cash, either. How many meals had she paid for with him? She'd lost count, and all hope she'd ever be reimbursed. It should have annoyed her a lot more, given that he was dripping in money. He simply forgot to bring any, and he usually ended up leaving his credit cards at home. Curse of traveling to dicey places, he'd explained, although she'd long thought he was just cheap.

The problem with Blake was that he always got away with it. She'd seen it over and over. People actually felt good about him leaching off them. Grown men who should know better. Women, well, she just figured they'd lost their good sense five minutes after meeting him. That never failed, either.

"What has you so angry?"

She looked up at him as she put the top back on the scotch. "I'm trying to figure out how much your no-good brother owes me. It's got to be in the thousands."

"Join the queue. I end up paying all kinds of people back, afraid he'll put a black mark on the family name."

"What am I, chopped liver?"

"What?"

She ignored both drinks as she rounded the bar. "You never pay me back."

"I always pay for the meals when the three of us go out."

"Oh. Right."

He gave her the eyebrow lift. Both brows. This expression she knew. "And how often do you and Blake eat together without me?"

"All the time. When we're in the same place, of course. He doesn't buy me dinner over the Internet or anything."

"Glad to hear it."

"What?"

"All the time?"

"Don't be ridiculous. I told you. Nothing ever happened between us. Just like nothing ever happened between *us*," she said.

His mouth opened in what she could only assume was righteous indignation. "That's how it should be. We're friends."

His phone rang. He stared at it for a several rapid heartbeats before he flipped it open. His eyes, right then, told her everything.

"Blake?"

Tears burned as Colin's face relaxed. Which meant Blake was safe. Not hurt. Not dead.

"You bloody moron," Colin shouted. "Where are you?" He cursed violently. "I can barely hear you. No, wait. Okay. Call me when you get a better line."

He held the phone tightly to his ear, but she could see he wasn't hearing anything. Finally, he flipped the thing closed, tossed it on the couch. "Thank God," he said, exhaling sharply.

"Do you know where he is?"

He shook his head. "Just that he's safe. The idiot."

Maggie smiled. "Yes, he is. Did he call your parents or are you in charge of that?"

"I think his boss is ringing them now, but I'll make sure they know." He still looked dazed, still a bit angry. Then he shoved a hand through his hair and the stoic mask fell into place. "Good. Now things can get back to normal."

Normal. The status quo. Only not for her. There would be no more dreams of a Broadway career. No more dreams of Colin falling in love with her. No more dreams at all.

He pulled her close for a hug, nothing more. But when she looked into his eyes, something snapped. And she kissed him.

5

THIS WAS CRAZY. She knew it was a mistake and she didn't care. He didn't love her, didn't want her. This was simply about raw emotion, relief that Blake was alive. But still, she kissed him. Even with her eyes closed, tears slipped down her cheeks, and she didn't care about that, either.

Then his lips parted, and, oh, God, he was kissing her back. His hands pulled her closer as he explored her mouth. Her heart pounded as she abandoned all restraint and showed him the truth. That she loved him, had loved him and that she always would.

His hands moved down her back, down the white Oxford shirt as he pressed his whole body against her. She gasped as she felt him harden, blushed even though she'd dreamed of him like this.

Still holding her tight, he pulled her with him as he moved back to the couch, lifting her legs so she straddled his lap. In a burst of surprise and delight, she used both fists to grab hold of his white shirt, and she kissed him again. Deeply. Passionately. Aggressively.

He met her just as eagerly. Could it be that she wasn't completely insane and that he wanted her, too?

It had been so long, and she'd been so sure it was hopeless. She'd tried to like someone else, anyone else, but it was only him. All these years, and…oh. His hand moved underneath her shirt and touched her bare back. He had the most beautiful hands, and they were touching her, finally, with need. She felt him tremble. All right, maybe that was her, but it could be both of them. His other hand came to join the first, but she couldn't bear to stop kissing him, not even to touch more than his chest.

Her body shivered as his fingers skimmed up her back. Pulling away, needing to breathe, she looked at him. His eyes opened. Dark, needy. And ashamed.

Oh, God.

Letting go of his shirt, she pushed him back against the couch, her heart thudding for a completely different reason.

He stretched, trying to kiss her again, but she climbed off him, took a couple of steps back.

His lips, still damp, parted. "Maggie?"

"Colin," she said, and it was her real voice. Not giddy with kisses and touching. "I'm sorry. That was a mistake. With Blake and all, I got carried away."

Instead of snapping out of his trance, he reached for her. "Please, Maggie, don't."

She didn't want to stop. She wanted all her fantasies to come true, but they were *fantasies*. He was just happy, that's all. Relieved that his twin was safe and she happened to be here. Responding because he was human and she'd practically attacked him.

But the truth had been in his eyes. "Colin, what do you want?"

"What?"

"What do you want from me?"

"I thought I was making myself pretty clear."

"Aside from sex. After. What then?"

"I know it was impetuous, and probably not the

smartest thing we've ever done, but Maggie, I care about you. You're my touchstone, my closest friend. But I really do find you attractive. I always have."

She pushed her hair back as she turned away. "I'm sorry. I don't know what got into me."

He came up behind her, put his hand on her shoulder. "Don't be sorry. Not for that. I'm not."

She plastered a smile on her face before she turned, dislodging his hand. "All right, then, I won't. Hey, didn't I pour us some drinks?" She spun around and went to the wet bar, but it was no use. She needed a moment alone, because her smile was going to crack into a thousand pieces. "I'll be back."

She used his bathroom, although she wished so hard she was at home. Her dress, covered in its thick, disgusting paste, looked almost as bad as she felt. Maggie sat down on the edge of his tub and curled her arms around her waist. She leaned over, trying like hell not to sob. He'd know. She wasn't one of those dainty things who let loose one solitary tear. She looked hideous when she really cried. Her face scrunched, her eyes got puffy and red. They probably already were from before.

The last thing she wanted was for things to go to hell before she moved. She still treasured his friendship, and with some distance, there was a real chance it could be just that. A friendship, on both sides. She didn't have anyone else, at least not a friendship that would stand the test of time. Being a military brat had made her wary of commitments, of making friends only to lose them. If she lost Colin, she'd be all alone.

He was right. He'd always been right. If they had sex, there was no telling what would happen between them. It was better not to know. Not to risk losing everything.

Tears threatened to fall again, and she pushed her palms against her eyes until she saw stars. When she could breathe without bursting, she looked at her hands, at the smudges of mascara.

Today was supposed to have been triumphant. The best day of her life.

A knock on the door made her grab on to the tub. "Yes?"

"You all right? Can I get you anything?"

"I'm fine, thanks. Just trying to get the dress clean. I'll be out in a minute."

There was no response and she relaxed. And then he spoke, stopping her heart again. "We should talk."

"I won't be long. Why don't you put on the kettle?"

"Good idea. Yes. I'll…I'll see you in the kitchen."

"Right."

She waited until she thought he must be gone, then she stood to take the few steps to the counter. It was clear the cornstarch hadn't had enough time to soak up the oil, but she didn't care. There was no way she was staying here. Not for the world. She'd done her duty as a friend, but now it was time for her to go home, where she could cry as hard as she wanted.

It took a long time to get the powder off the dress, and it was a horrible job. The oil remained, but now it was a white paste. It didn't matter. She had her coat, and if she couldn't wear this dress again, so be it.

Taking off his shirt was terribly bittersweet. She folded it neatly, even though she knew he was going to have it cleaned. Then she put her dress back on, not willing to look at the mess in the mirror.

Finally, after washing her hands and wiping off the smudges under her eyes, she opened the door. Following a couple of deep breaths, she went quietly into the

living room, to the couch where she'd put her coat and
boots. Slipping them on as silently as possible, she put
her heels into her bag, and went to face him.

He stood at the counter, leaning on his hands as he
stared out the window.

"Colin."

He spun around. For a second, he looked hurt. But
no, not him. Worried, maybe, but not hurt. "You're
leaving?"

"I need to go. You haven't slept in ages. And you
need to call your parents. Besides, it's getting late. I
have to get ready."

"Ready?"

"Just one of the things I forgot to tell you," she said,
not sure why she was saying it even as the words left
her lips. "I've got a date for New Year's."

"You don't. We talked about it. Before."

"You assumed I didn't, Colin, and no wonder. I
haven't been getting out nearly enough. And then
Jeffrey, you know, from the IT department, he asked and
I said yes."

"Jeffrey?"

She had no idea why she'd picked him. He was pleasant and not awkward for an IT guy, but she wasn't
remotely interested in him. "He's smart and funny, too.
And I have to figure out what I'm going to wear." She
waved her free hand as if it were no big deal. "You'll
be all right, won't you?"

"Me?" He didn't answer for a long time. "Yes. Yes,
I'll be fine. Wait. You said this was one of the things you
forgot to tell me. What was the other?"

She stopped cold. It took her a moment to regroup.
Right. Weeks ago, when she'd first gotten the offer,
she'd told him there was a possible promotion in her

future. She hadn't mentioned anything about the new job requiring her to move to D.C. Because there'd been the hope. The dream. But there had been no audition. And now the only thing she had left was the opportunity to advance her career.

It was the time to tell him. Now that she knew for certain there was no hope left with him, either.

The kettle whistled and he jerked the knob on the stove so hard she thought it might break.

"About that." She cleared her throat. "You know the promotion I spoke to you about? I've decided to accept the position. It'll take a while for the paperwork to go through so it's not as if I'll be leaving that soon, but—"

"Leaving?" He stared at her, confusion clouding his features. "What do you mean?"

"The job is in the D.C. office."

"No."

She shrugged. "It's not that far."

"Christ, Maggie." His lips thinned. He looked angry. "When were you going to tell me?"

"I didn't know for sure until today."

He narrowed his gaze. "Today?"

"No, no, it's got nothing to do with—" She knew what he was thinking and she didn't want him to presume she was moving because of that kiss. She looked away for a moment. "I promised myself that if the audition didn't pan out, it was time for me to get serious about my career."

As her words registered, he looked as if someone had punched him in the stomach, and then he muttered a word she'd never heard him use.

She had to get out of here. "Anyway, Happy New Year, Colin. I'm glad everything worked out so well."

"Right." He walked her to the front door, but didn't open it.

"When you speak to Blake again, tell him not to be such an idiot."

He said nothing. Didn't even smile.

She stared down at her feet. "Happy New Year, Colin. Oh, I already said that."

"Maggie—"

"It's going to be hell getting a cab." She flung open the door and hurried down the hall, more anxious to get out of there than she'd thought possible. Thankfully, the elevator was on his floor. She stepped inside, and the moment the doors were shut, she fell back against the wall. But she wouldn't cry yet. Not yet.

6

COLIN SHUT THE DOOR and leaned his head against the wood. What the hell was going on? He felt as if he'd been hit over the head and wasn't quite out of his coma. Maggie was moving away. And she'd kissed him. Not just any kiss, but a kiss that had knocked him for a considerable loop. And she'd been crying.

He started toward the kitchen, but segued to the bar instead where he picked up his scotch. After a healthy swig, he put his glass down, absolutely perplexed. Why wouldn't she tell him the job wasn't in New York? It made no sense. They spoke about most things, almost everything, and moving to D.C. was hardly insignificant.

He went back to the couch, drink in hand. *Doctor Who* was still on, but a different episode. He looked away, stared instead at the carpet by the ottoman where she'd spilled the oil. Lord, the way she'd looked in his shirt. It wasn't any wonder he'd reacted to her kiss. He wasn't stupid, and it wasn't as if he hadn't given the question serious thought. Blake had told him to go for it. In fact, he'd said Colin was a bloody imbecile if he didn't.

But if she wanted them to be more than friends, she would have said something before now, wouldn't she? He'd have picked up on it. There had been moments. Looks. The occasional sigh, but nothing concrete. Besides, she was dating this Jeffrey person.

Dammit. She'd raced out of here as if she never wanted to see him again. Bizarre that two of his worst fears would come to haunt him on the same day. One had turned out as well as anything concerning his brother could, but something told him Maggie's story would not.

Had she ever mentioned Jeffrey before? He didn't think so. Perhaps he'd forgotten, although that seemed unlikely. He'd always had a vested interest in the men in Maggie's life. She had no family here in New York, and he'd taken it upon himself to be her sort of big brother. She'd teased him about it, but he thought he'd done a rather good job.

So why hadn't she spoken of Jeffrey before? Was she trying to hide him? Did she already know that he'd find fault?

Colin sipped his drink, his mind whirling with unsavory possibilities. Nowadays, even someone vetted for Homeland Security could be hiding things. A drug habit, a gambling problem. Maybe he liked to tie women up or…

His eyes closed as vivid pictures swam to his mind, not of some faceless man but of himself, touching the skin of her back. Kissing her. Feeling her body pressed to his.

Dammit. No. He was supposed to look after her, and now all he could think of was the taste of her. No matter what, he was still Maggie's friend. That entailed responsibilities he wasn't going to forgo even if she hated him for making her miss her audition. And he had made her. He should never have called. He'd known about it for weeks. He'd even encouraged her to break a leg.

Maggie being Maggie, she'd come to his rescue. No wonder she wanted to leave.

He stood, polished off his drink and made up his

mind. She hadn't been gone that long, and if he hurried, he might still be able to talk to her before she left for the night. He'd be able to check out her date, as well.

This had to be played smartly, though. He'd apologize and make sure they were square, and if he thought for one second that Jeffrey wasn't the right sort... Well, he wouldn't want to cheat her out of a New Year's extravaganza. He would take her to the embassy party. She'd like that. He should have asked her a month ago.

He got out his black suit. He'd have his cell with him in case Blake called, but he must hurry and get to Maggie's before it was too late.

MAGGIE LOOKED AT HER dress, puddled on the floor of her bathroom, right next to the huge pile of tear-drenched tissues in the bin. She should put some more cornstarch on the stain and hope for the best, but she didn't have the energy or the desire. Screw the dress. Screw everything.

She shuffled to her bedroom, which seemed tinier than ever. Uglier, too. Why had she ever moved here? She should never have gone to Cambridge or accepted the job in New York. She should have gone to a community college. Gotten married, like her friend Liz, and had a bunch of kids. Whatever happened to Liz? They'd been so close that one year in high school. Liz had been a lot of fun, until she'd hooked up with what's his name. Until Maggie had moved, yet again.

She let her bra and panties drop where she stood and pulled on her flannel cowboy pajama bottoms and the yellow sleep shirt that had the pomegranate stain. It didn't matter anyway. No one was going to see her. It wasn't as if she really had a date.

Now she had a big decision to make. Alcohol or Ben

& Jerry's? She'd already started on her way to mind-lessness, so alcohol made sense. But the ice cream was that one with chocolate chunks. No contest.

She slipped into her big fuzzy slippers and shuffled through what she called her all-purpose room, but was actually three-quarters of the apartment she'd sectioned off into living room, dining room and kitchen. It used to make her laugh that the whole place would have fit into Colin's bedroom. Tonight, she didn't give a damn. All she wanted was a spoon.

In the kitchen, she got just that, then stopped as her gaze hit the bottle of Baileys she'd been given for Christmas. Inspiration struck. She got out her largest tumbler and made herself a Ben & Jerry's and Baileys float. Brilliant.

With her spoon and a straw in the glass, she curled up on her couch, which was actually a love seat, and turned on the television.

There was *Doctor Who*. Excellent. The marathon continued. Double excellent. Legs crossed, tears dry, looking almost as bad as she felt, she turned up the sound, hoping against hope that sometime during the night, she'd pass out and not wake up for six months.

THE CAB SITUATION WAS intolerable. All of them were full and there were dozens of doormen whistling them down, his included. Colin debated walking, but the streets were equally insane.

Everyone, it seemed, had decided that midnight was only a suggestion and that celebrations should begin hours earlier. Knowing Jeffrey, he was that sort of buffoon. IT tech indeed. There had to be something wrong with him or Maggie would have mentioned him earlier. The man was probably going to take her to a *Star*

Trek convention or something just as appalling. She'd be mortified and end up calling him anyway, so it was best to put an end to this farce right now.

The doorman blew his whistle again, agitatedly waving at every cab, including the gypsies, clearly having caught on to Colin's desperation.

It was no use. He handed Sonny a twenty for his trouble, and he was off. His wool coat masterfully kept out the biting air, but could do nothing for his face. The icy wind regaled him with staggering gusts, but he pressed on, dodging revelers and those who had already reached their destination of complete oblivion.

Most days, this route was pleasant and colorful. He liked his neighborhood and often walked through it. Tonight, he cursed each crosswalk and stoplight, each brightly festooned shop and every high-heeled woman who mocked him by clinging to her date, laughing at unfunny jokes.

She couldn't have left yet. She had to choose something to wear, she'd said, and that took time. Damn, but he was glad he'd ruined that red dress. The thought of her wearing it for someone else…

God, what the bloody hell was wrong with him?

He nearly ran down a teenage couple too busy kissing to see where they were going, but sidestepped them just in time. They glared at him as if he were the culprit. He tugged up his collar in deference to the cold and thought of calling her, but he was afraid she wouldn't answer when she saw his name. Even worse, that she'd tell him to leave her alone and mind his own business.

That was the point—Maggie *was* his business. They were a team. They looked out for each other. She was always there when he needed her, and he did his damndest to be there for her.

That had been one of the problems between him and Elizabeth, hadn't it? Neither of them had put the other first, and didn't that prove Maggie's friendship was worth fighting for? And didn't a friend stop a friend from going out with the shady computer jockey who was probably installing spyware on her laptop right this second?

His phone vibrated in his pocket and he stopped to pull it out. Blake, not Maggie. He flipped it on. "Blake."

"I finally got a connection that's decent. Talked to Mother and Dad, now you, but it's got to be short because I still haven't slept."

"What happened to you?"

"Lost the equipment. Had to bribe an unreasonable guard. It was bollocks, but I got the story and I wasn't shot."

"Good, that's— Excuse me, I'm trying to cross the street here."

"Where are you?" Blake asked.

"On my way to see Maggie."

"I thought she was at your flat."

"It seems you're not the only one I have to worry about. She's off on a date with someone I don't trust as far as I can throw him."

"Oh? Who's that?"

"Jeffrey. He works at Homeland."

"What's wrong with him?"

"Just a minute." Colin shoved out his arm as he saw a cab with the light on. "Stop, there. Taxi!" The cab sped by, and he brought the phone back up to his ear. "What?"

"Who is this guy? A serial killer?"

"I don't know. That's the problem. She didn't even tell me about him until she left."

"So you've never met him?"

"I'm about to. There's no way I'm letting her go out, tonight of all nights, with someone like him."

Blake laughed. Really laughed. As hard as he did at his own jokes.

"What's so damn funny?"

"Jesus, Colin. I'm sorry I worried you. Go to your Maggie. Put your foot down. And Colin. Don't be an idiot."

"That's what Maggie told me to tell you."

"Well, that makes its own kind of sense. Now run, you fool. Run!"

Colin snapped his phone shut and took his brother's advice. He wasn't that far now. He just had to make it before Jeffrey.

MAGGIE TOOK ANOTHER PULL at her Baileys float. It was almost finished, and that wouldn't do. She'd make another. And if that didn't make her drunk enough, another after that. It helped that it hardly tasted of booze.

Dammit. There was another episode of *Doctor Who* coming on, and she hadn't caught the end of the last one. Oh, well. It was a repeat, and she owned all the DVDs.

Colin had introduced her to *Doctor Who*. He'd been a fan for years, and he'd been so enthusiastic she'd had to watch the new series. They'd made a point of watching it together.

The jerk didn't even know she loved him. Had loved him forever. He treated her as if he were her brother, a strict brother at that. For a guy who was just supposed to be her friend, he sure cared a lot about who she dated.

Why couldn't that kiss have been the real thing? Was

that too much to ask? It had felt as real as anything, but his eyes had told her the truth. Great. So he wouldn't throw her out of bed. That's not what she wanted. She loved him.

Oh, crap. The truth was, she'd spent the past six years of her life living in the world of magical thinking. If she could only get a part on Broadway, then she'd be happy. If only Colin loved her the way she loved him, then she would feel alive, be complete. All hopes and dreams and pie in the sky and all of it a waste. It was time to stop. Just stop. Cold turkey. She'd leave more than this horrible apartment behind. No more pining away. No more singing lessons or acting classes. And no more Colin.

Really, who did he think he was, questioning her about her love life? She could go out with whomever she wanted. Take Jeffrey. He was probably a wonderful guy. Her unconscious had pulled him up for some reason, right? He was more than likely her destiny. The man who would sweep her off her feet. Although he was a little chubby to literally sweep her, but metaphorically, he was probably a regular Romeo. Only older, and not into poison and better with computers.

She spooned out the last bits of ice cream. She didn't even get dizzy as she went the five steps into her kitchen to fix another.

Just as she was about to pour the Baileys in the glass, someone banged on her door. It was loud and urgent. Crap, the building was probably on fire. It would be just her luck tonight. This old rattrap was bound to go down in flames.

"Just a minute!" She grabbed the blanket off the couch, slung it around her shoulders, then threw open the door.

7

OF ALL THE POSSIBLE scenarios that had run through Colin's head on coming over here, Maggie looking like a crazed beggar woman hadn't occurred once. He had no response to this. In fact, he thought his head might just explode.

"What the hell?" she said, her voice somewhere between affronted and furious.

"What the hell indeed."

"What are you doing here?"

He shook his head, trying to clear it. "What are you doing here?"

"Quit repeating what I'm saying."

"I have no words."

"Clearly."

"Where's Jeffrey?"

"What?"

He took a step inside. "Where's Jeffrey?" he asked again, only louder.

"He's late. Why are you here?"

"Late?" Colin took another step to look inside. There was hardly reason to. The whole apartment could fit on the head of a pin. "You going to a costume ball?"

"What's it to you?" she asked, pulling her god-awful throw tighter over her stained T-shirt.

"You never mentioned him before. I want to know what you're playing at."

"Tough. I don't recall asking for your opinion."

"Too bad. I'm going to give it anyway."

With a loud huff, Maggie slammed the door shut. "I don't want you here."

"Then why'd you close the door?"

She put both hands out as if she were choking him. "Go home, Colin. This is not your business."

"You are my business."

"Why? Why do you care who I date? You don't even care who Blake dates and he really is your brother."

"You're different."

"But why? And if you say it's because I'm a girl, I'll castrate you myself."

That made him stop. And think. He stared at her for a long while, her face a blotchy mess, her clothes a horror, and it didn't matter. Nothing she could do would matter. "You're my friend. I care about you."

"Oh, go to hell," she said, the cold in her voice as shocking as the words.

"What?"

"You heard me. Go to hell, you and your friendship. Did it ever occur to you that I don't want to be your friend? That being your friend is too goddamn hard? It's done. It's over. I want you to leave right now. And don't call me. Ever."

She choked on that last word and her face utterly fell apart. She covered herself with her hands, but there was no way to mask her sobs.

Colin's heart twisted with her pain and his own. He had no idea what the devil was going on, but this was unbearable. He pulled her into his arms and held her tight, wanting to make it better.

She didn't mean what she'd said. She couldn't. It was all madness, and his fault for always expecting her to be there for him. Selfish bastard. If only he'd thought. She wouldn't be so angry with him and she wouldn't be crying.

"Shh," he whispered, rocking her. "It'll be all right."

She pushed his chest, forcing him to let her go. When she looked up at him there was such pain in her eyes. "I know," she said so softly he barely heard her. "Please, just go."

His thoughts were everywhere and nowhere, and he couldn't make a cogent argument for staying. Then again, he couldn't leave. "No."

"Please don't make this harder." She opened the door for him and stood with her head down.

Neither of them moved. A door shut somewhere down the hall. Horns honked outside. He couldn't hear her breathe or see if she was still crying, and everything in him told him if he left now his whole world would come crashing down.

She was right. He didn't care about Blake's love life. Well, he did, but in a totally different way. The thought of Maggie being with someone got to him as few other things did. Someone unworthy, that is.

Someone…else.

"Oh, shit," he said.

Maggie looked up.

"I'm a complete idiot," he said.

"I know."

He closed the door with his elbow as he took her by the shoulders. "A bloody fool."

"I know."

"That's why… Elizabeth was… Even Blake said—"

"Colin?"

He looked at her crossly. "Why on earth didn't you tell me?"

"Tell you what?"

"That I'm in love with you."

Her mouth opened and her puffy eyes widened as much as they could. "Oh."

"I've loved you all this time."

She swallowed and blinked. "All this…" Her head drooped for a long moment, and then she met his gaze again. "Colin?"

"Yes?"

"Either you kiss me right now or I swear to God…"

When he let go of her arms, Maggie wrapped them around his neck and they met with a kiss that changed everything. He loved her. He'd loved her as long as she'd loved him. He was an idiot, but he was her idiot. He loved her.

HIS LIPS SMOTHERED ANY other thought and she didn't care what she looked like, or that her ice cream was melting, because this was crazy wonderful.

She found herself lifted straight up off the floor and her legs wrapped around his hips as he carried her, still ravishing her mouth, straight back to the bedroom, to her ridiculous little bed.

He put her down. Looking at him, she could see her own amazement echoed on his face, in his smile. She threw off the blanket and pulled off her sleep shirt. By the time it was over her head, his jacket was on the floor and his shirt was half-unbuttoned. He'd left her no room to stand so she got hold of his waistband and undid the button. He stopped her at the zipper. "I'd better do that."

She understood when she saw it wasn't a straight line down. Considerably.

Instead, she shimmied out of her pajama bottoms, which she tossed away with her foot. Her aim wasn't all that great as they landed mostly on his head.

Hearing him laugh was like icing on a cupcake. Watching him strip was more of an adult entertainment, but just as sweet.

As if they'd done this a hundred times, he climbed on the bed and scooped her into his arms. She'd wanted to be naked with Colin for so long that she closed her eyes and wiggled her whole body against his.

He cried out, and she froze. "What?"

"Nothing. Wonderful. Surprising."

"Ah, well, then that's all right."

"Very much so."

She couldn't help it. She loved that he would say "very much so" when his dick was pointing to his chin. "Don't ever stop being just like you are," she said.

He kissed her bare shoulder. "I have no idea what you're talking about."

"I know. I want to totally jump your bones, but the condoms are in the bathroom."

He deflated—not his dick, his chest. "All the way over there?"

"You could probably reach by stretching."

"If only." He kissed her and then stood up, still waving his flag. "I'll be back in a moment."

"That would be charming," she said, very politely in her best British accent.

"You mock me, but you Americans have butchered a perfectly fine language."

"Really? You want to talk linguistics? Now?"

"Point taken." He hurried to the bathroom, giving her a nice look at his naked rear. If all those women from the embassy knew what was hiding under those wool suits, there would be a line outside his door.

He was back in a flash with the whole box. "I can't find the expiration date."

She laughed. Only Colin would be so bloody sensible. "It's sometime this year. We're fine."

A brilliant smile made her insides twitch. "I was joking. Now, where was I?"

"About to be jumped."

He climbed on the bed again. She, leaning up on her elbows, laughed at how his feet hung off the bed. "We should have thought this through. Gone back to your place."

"The hell. I want you. Now."

She melted back down to her pillow. "Oh, you just keep getting better."

He was above her, looking down into her eyes. "So badly."

She kissed him, long and slow, her hands on either side of his head. This would be their first time, but only the first. They had all the time in the world to make love in every way they could imagine.

He flopped down beside her, on his back. "I'd better—"

She brought out a condom from the box on the bed. "Let me."

He smiled and his cock jumped.

"Oh, look, it's excited."

"Don't you dare name it."

"What?"

He sighed. "Nothing."

She ripped the package open, then straddled his legs. She knew how to do this, even though it had been a while, but first, before there was all that latex, she wanted something more personal.

Sliding down a bit, she leaned over and took the base in her hand, holding him steady. Then, with a wicked grin, she licked him straight up all the way to the crown. She swirled her tongue to the sound of him gasping, to the feel of him thrusting, then holding steady.

"What's wrong?"

"Maggie, love, if you do that again, it'll be a while until we truly get the show on the road."

"It might be worth it."

"I want to be inside you."

She didn't argue. Carefully, not even daring to breathe, she sheathed him in the condom, already anxious for when they wouldn't have to go through this nonsense.

He tugged at her arms, and she expected him to throw her down on the bed. Instead, he pulled her up to her knees and then, with his hands cupping her ass, he lifted her until she was centered above him. Like they'd been on the couch.

"Why, Mr. Griffith. You surprise me."

"There's more to me than meets the eye."

She looked down and took hold of him once more. "Obviously."

No more teasing. She couldn't wait. Closing her eyes, she slid down, but not too much. Just enough to feel the crown slip inside.

He groaned, but he didn't buck. His left hand squeezed her thigh and his right palm brushed against her already hard nipple.

Clever man, that almost ruined her plan. But still, she moved her hips up and back, teasing them both.

"You're going to kill me," he said, his voice as tight as his muscles.

"Not yet." She moved lower by inches, stopping just until she could relax fully, then she'd go deeper. When there were still a few more inches to go, she couldn't stand it anymore. She sank down all the way, letting him fill her, loving being filled.

"Oh, God, Maggie."

He bucked, and she held on.

It wasn't nearly as quick as she'd feared. He surprised her again when he flipped her to the bottom, when he positioned her so perfectly that his cock not only went deep, but brushed against her clit with every push.

And yet it was his kiss that tipped her over the edge. Which was no surprise at all.

8

THEY WERE UNDER THE covers now, and after some deft maneuvering of bent knees and make-do cuddling, his whole body was on the bed and he felt better than he had in years. That he could touch her, that she wanted him to touch her, was incredible.

It didn't hurt that she was touching him back.

Outside noises bled into the room, but weren't enough to bother. In some foolish part of his brain, he wanted to think all the rejoicing was in their honor. Why had he thought keeping Maggie at arm's length was a good idea? The irony stung. So afraid of losing her that he'd nearly lost her. Not to mention wasted so much time on his rationalizations.

"One hell of a day," she said.

"What?"

"I said, this has been one hell of a day. Did you speak to Blake?"

"Briefly."

"So he really is all right."

"Yes. He is. I would think he's in hot water with the honchos at BBC, but he's alive and fit."

"He's always in hot water."

"Usually with a few beautiful women."

She ran her fingernails gently down the length of

his penis. He inhaled sharply and tweaked her nipple as a thank-you.

"I didn't know you had a thing for cowgirl style," she said, her smile evident in her voice.

"I didn't, either. What's cowgirl style?"

She laughed. "Me on top. You know, waving the metaphorical cowboy hat, shouting yippee-ki-yay."

He lifted his head to stare at her. "You have no idea how many things I want to do with you."

"Can't wait to find out."

His head landed on the pillow again as his hand brushed down to her stomach. Her skin was soft as silk, and he very much liked the sweet, small V of her pubic hair. Altogether perfect. "It's because I'm British, isn't it? Our reputations aren't quite on par with the French or Italians."

"Mmm. I've always known you were polite on the outside and a wild man in private."

"I'm not that polite."

"Ooo, yummy."

He smiled, but cogent thought was returning and there were things to say. "Now, about Jeffrey—"

She coughed and blushed. "He's a very nice man I know from work. But he wasn't my date. I just wanted you to think I wasn't dateless on New Year's."

Colin snorted. All that worry and he wasn't even real. "What about moving to D.C.?"

Her voice sobered. "That's very real. I'd put off telling them my answer until after the audition. Can't put it off any longer, though."

"I'm sorry about all of that," he said.

"All of what?"

"Calling you. I knew how important today was, and I should never have asked you to come. I stole your big dream."

"It's all right. I suppose I could have gone to the audition, then come to you if it was that important to me. There was honestly no place I'd have rather been. I love you. Which begs the question."

"What question is that?"

"It's midnight."

"That's not a question."

"We're starting an entirely new year. And, well, this." She waved her hand vaguely over the two of them.

As he petted her and let his fingers slide where they would, he thought about what she meant. Everything had changed. He not only had his closest friend, he had his lover. In his arms. But she wouldn't be living in New York and that was a problem. One he could solve. "I'll change home base to D.C. Take the commuter flight along with everyone else. It'll be better."

She snuggled closer. "What do you mean, better?"

"This will be the year you're mine."

She sighed. "I like the sound of that."

"Now I have a question."

"What's that?"

"Why didn't you say anything? If you felt this way, we could have—"

She sighed. "You were so afraid that we'd fall apart. I guess I was afraid, too. I didn't want anything to happen to us. So I sublimated. Stupid, huh?"

"No. This was all on me. I was rather insistent, wasn't I? But you're the most important person in my life. You know that, right?"

"Yes. I've known that for a long time. Maybe that's why I couldn't let it go. It wasn't easy, though. I was ready to throw in the towel."

"I'm glad you kissed me. I think I knew then. That moment. It was a revelation."

"It could have gone more smoothly."

Unable to help himself, he pulled her closer and let himself luxuriate. "You're right. It could have. Suppose we make up for it now."

He held her steady as he took her mouth. Kissing Maggie was unlike anything he'd experienced before. She stole his breath and his sense and all he wanted was more.

Simply feeling her naked body had him wanting her again and even when he tried to slow things down, to let himself linger at her lips, he couldn't stop moving against her. Soft, pliant, her body moved with him as he slid one hand down between her legs.

She pulled back. "Wait...don't...stop," she said, gasps coming between each word.

He stilled his finger. "Do you want me to wait or not?"

Maggie laughed. "I want to get the condom, and I was afraid I'd get carried away."

He closed his eyes and couldn't help but laugh, as well. "This bed is too small. We'll need to get a large flat in D.C."

She had just kissed his chin and that's where she stayed for several long breaths. He didn't move, either, not quite sure what was happening.

"You want us to move in together?"

"Yes. I'd like to come home to you at night, and wake up to you in the morning."

She pushed him backward, luckily not off the bed. "You don't think it's a bit sudden? I mean, don't you need time to get used to all this? To me?"

"We've already wasted too much time."

"Living together is a big deal," she said finally. "You like being on your own, you've told me that."

He touched her beautiful cheek. "I'm already used to

putting your bourbon and 7-Up in the cupboard. I stock your awful cookies. You're already converted to the cult of *Doctor Who*. Besides, we won't be moving into my place. It'll be ours. And you'll have to get used to me."

"Wow."

"If you want to, that is."

She nodded, looking a bit dazed. "I want to."

"Perhaps it wouldn't be presumptuous, then, to tell you I want these things for a long time to come?"

After a few deep breaths she smiled. "Let me see if I can translate that to American." She furrowed her brow and bit her lower lip enticingly. "You want this to last for the rest of our lives?"

"I do. Now that I've seen it, I can't see anything else. I love you. I want you."

She kissed him squarely and deeply. When she pulled back, she whispered, "My miracle."

"What's that?"

Maggie shook her head. "Nothing. Just… I'm happy. Tomorrow we'll sit down and talk about what's next, okay? I want us both rational and thoughtful. But for the rest of January 1, I don't want to think about anything but making love. Agreed?"

He kissed the tip of her nose. "Absolutely." Then he closed his eyes as he kissed her lips, swept in to taste her again. It wasn't simply the first day of the year, but the first day of his real life. The life they were meant to share.

* * * * *

TOO HOT TO HANDLE & PLAY WITH ME
(2-IN-1 ANTHOLOGY)
BY NANCY WARREN & LESLIE KELLY

Too Hot to Handle

Lexy, an up-and-coming jewellery designer, discovers a passion for a 'thief', who has stolen her heart and has no plans to return it.

Play With Me

When two opposites attract and go to Vegas, they get more than they bargained for, dodging their internet fans and trying to figure out how they feel about each other!

WANTED!
BY VICKI LEWIS THOMPSON

Photographer Dominique is dying to break loose and live a little. And seducing shirtless, earthy cowboy Nick looks like just the place to start...

WHILE SHE WAS SLEEPING...
BY ISABEL SHARPE

Sawyer is convinced Alana is missing out on all the fun and substance of life, sacrificing herself to family duty. He does everything he can think of to seduce her into realising what she's missing...

**On sale from 21st January 2011
Don't miss out!**

*Available at WHSmith, Tesco, ASDA, Eason
and all good bookshops*

www.millsandboon.co.uk

0111/14

THE *Royal*
HOUSE OF NIROLI

*The richest royal family in the world—united by blood
and passion, torn apart by deceit and desire*

The Royal House of Niroli: Scandalous Seductions
Penny Jordan & Melanie Milburne
Available 17th December 2010

The Royal House of Niroli: Billion Dollar Bargains
Carol Marinelli & Natasha Oakley
Available 21st January 2011

The Royal House of Niroli: Innocent Mistresses
Susan Stephens & Robyn Donald
Available 18th February 2011

The Royal House of Niroli: Secret Heirs
Raye Morgan & Penny Jordan
Available 18th March 2011

Collect all four!